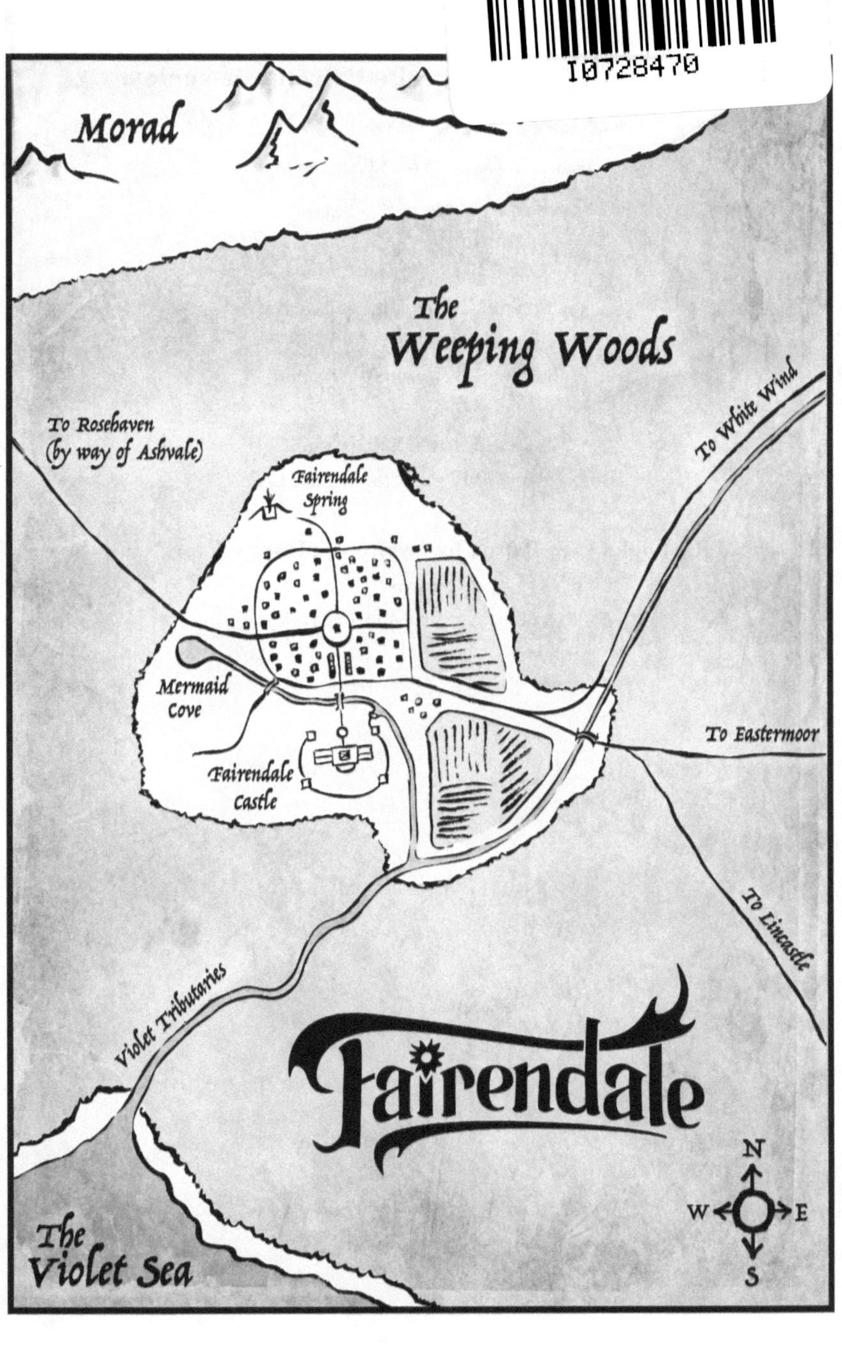

Morad
The Weeping Woods
To Rosehaven
(by way of Ashvale)
To White Wind
Fairendale Spring
Mermaid Cove
To Eastermoor
Fairendale Castle
To Lincastle
Violet Tributaries
Fairendale
The Violet Sea
N
W
E
S

Read all the books in the Fairendale series!

Book .5: *The Good King's Fall (a prequel)*
Book 1: *The Treacherous Secret*
Book 2: *The King's Pursuit*
Book 3: *The Perilous Crossing*
Book 4: *The Dragons of Morad*
Book 5: *The Fiery Aftermath*
Book 6: *The Mysterious Separation*

Collector's Editions:
Books 1-6: *The Flight of the Magical Children*

To see all the books L.R. Patton has written, please click or visit the link below:
www.lrpatton.com/store

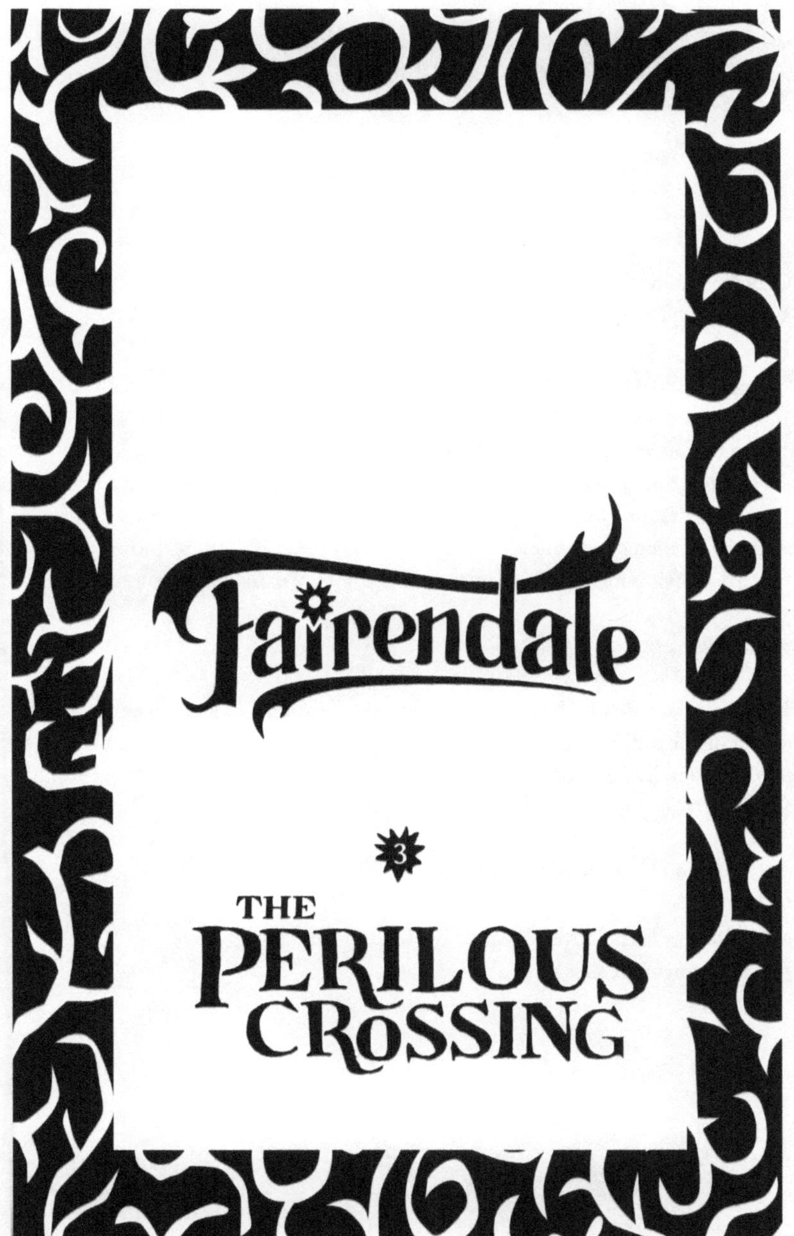

Fairendale

3

THE PERILOUS CROSSING

Batlee Press
PO Box 591596
San Antonio, TX 78259

This is a work of fiction. Names, characters, places and incidents are either the product of the author's imagination or are used fictitiously, and any resemblance to actual persons, living or dead, business establishments, events or locales is entirely coincidental.

Printed in the United States of America

First Edition—2016/Cover designed by Toalson Marketing
www.toalsonmarketing.com

L.R. PATTON

THE PERILOUS CROSSING

BATLEE PRESS

*To the ones
who made me
brave enough
to try*

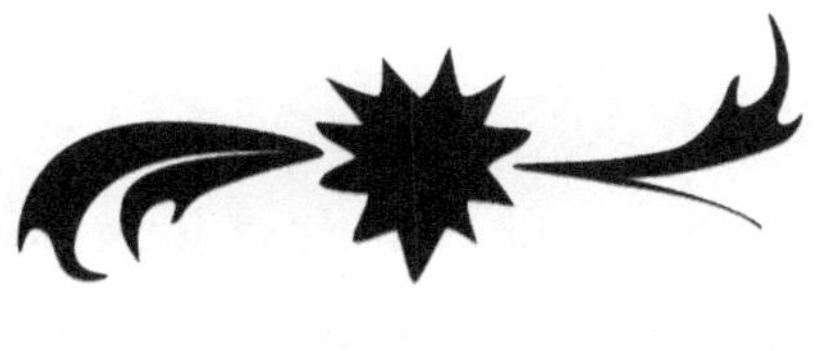

Love

Maude and Arthur tried to save the children, and now they have failed. They have failed in all the ways that matter, in all the ways that end in children staying alive. They do not know where their son is. Their daughter is, daily, losing the strength of her gift, for every day she spends without the brother born mere minutes after she was is another day her magic weakens, at the risk of vanishing. The other children are hungry, thirsty, weak, unable to summon magic as well, for when children hunger, magic does not obey.

Magic has its rules, after all.

And now they are trapped beneath the earth, while the world moves on and they ration what food they have and watch it, still, diminish. They are no closer to finding a solution than they were before, though it has, in truth, been only a day since they discovered themselves trapped beneath the ground in a secret hiding place that no one, now, will ever be able to find, for there is no longer a portal leading back to the land above. It feels, to the children, that they have been trapped beneath the earth for weeks.

Whatever will they do?

Arthur knows they will not exist long without food and, especially, without Mercy's ability to draw water from the ground, for she has grown far too weak. They have done what they can, kept the food portions small, turned everything they have into more food, but it is the water that confounds him. Mercy, you see, is the most powerful among his students, particularly since his daughter's magic has, in effect, dried up outside the presence of her twin brother Theo, who disappeared in the king's roundup, but even Mercy struggles to bring drops into the cup a girl named Ursula holds against the dirt.

"Come," Ursula says. "You must try again."

Arthur watches Mercy lower her staff to the place where the cup meets dirt, watches her eyes glaze, looks at the way her flaming red hair has grown dull in her hiding. He takes a deep breath. He looks at his wife. "Enough," he says.

Mercy drops to the ground. Maude, Arthur's pale wife, moves to lift the girl onto a chair. Mercy does not sit, though, so much as she slumps.

"But what shall we do, Father?" Hazel says. Her eyes, once

the color of a spring morning sky, are now the color of fog. She is graying. They are all graying. Arthur cannot bear it. They will die, trapped beneath the very land they love.

"Hush, child," Maude says. It is unclear whether she is speaking to her daughter or the girl who sobs in her arms.

"We shall rest," Arthur says. "We shall rest for a time. Then we shall try again."

"But we need water," says one of the boys, Chester, a trickster among the group who plays tricks no longer. One can understand, perhaps, that the reality of finding oneself trapped beneath the earth with no way out leaves no room for trickery and games. His twin brother, Charles, who has always been a quiet sort where his brother was loud, puts a hand on his brother's arm, as if to stop the words after they have already met the ears of all those gathered in the room.

There are twenty-four children squeezed in this underground home, along with Maude and Arthur. They hide for their lives. They hide, they believe, right alongside Death, though we, dear reader, can see that he is not here at all.

You see, a tiny shoe was found on the outside. A shoe that held a very large portal that has, now, been broken. Their way out no longer exists.

"We shall find water," Arthur says. He puts on a brave face for the children, for Arthur has always been the hopeful sort. His wife, however, knows him better. She sees the uncertainty that hides in the wrinkle between his eyebrows. She knows what certainty they face.

"Rest, Mercy," Maude says to the girl still shaking in her arms. "It is the best thing you can do for now."

The children grow silent. The candlelight wavers around them all, huddled in a tiny kitchen carved from the earth. Maude has put a pot on the fire with the last of the water. She will fill it with the last of the vegetables so they can have something to eat, though it will not be much.

Maude looks around. So many children. So many faces. So many eyes looking desperately for a way out. Maude shivers, though it is anything but cold in this room beneath the ground. Arthur crosses the room to her side.

"We have some food stored away," he says. She looks at this man who is her husband, this man who has seen her through every other danger in their lives. Surely he will be able to get them out of this one. Arthur looks at her and knows what she is thinking. It is not an easy knowing, this one, that someone depends on you to pull a miracle from wherever it is miracles come.

Their eyes hold for a moment, and then Maude says, "Not nearly enough. Not nearly enough to live for long. We must find a way out."

"Yes," Arthur says, gazing back toward the children. "We must." He clears his throat. "In the meantime, we shall live as long as we can. Let the children eat first. They need their strength."

"No," Hazel says, for she has been listening to her parents, along with the others, for children know how to listen without seeming to. "We all eat, or none of us eat."

Was there ever a braver child who lived than this Hazel? She cannot imagine a life without Maude and Arthur, the mother and father she has always admired and trusted and, most of all, loved. She knows that if they do not eat, they die, and if they die, the children shall die. All of them, for no one knows as much about magic as Arthur and Maude, though they cannot themselves practice it.

Hazel thinks of her brother, Theo. She knows he is not dead. She can feel it. He is out there somewhere. Perhaps he will find them. She knows, dear reader, that this is quite a fantastical hope, but hope does not always listen to reason.

"Yes, we all eat," the children say, murmuring their agreement, for they know what little chance they have without Arthur and Maude.

"Perhaps I could crawl out?" says a tiny boy named Tom, whose shoe was used to create the portal that has been broken. He is the size of a thumb, so small the children must watch their steps always. "Perhaps I could crawl through the cracks in the earth."

"And I," says a tiny girl named Thumbelina, whom the children call Lina. She steps forward. Her blue dress is so small it looks as if it is a scrap of fabric, which it likely is, for her mother and father were very poor, and stitches this small are very hard to make, though one might argue it would take only a few stitches to make a dress to fit a girl so tiny.

"And what would you do when you escape?" Chester says. "Dig us all out?"

They grow quiet once again, though it was Chester's attempt to make light of the situation in which they find themselves. The children though, including Chester, feel that the situation is anything but light. Laughter does not exist in this hole beneath the ground. Perhaps it once did, before a soldier of the king stumbled, with quite extraordinary luck, we might all agree, upon the tiny shoe and carried away to King Willis what link Arthur, Maude, and the children had to the outside world. But now, well. It is a somber mood that settles upon the place.

"It is too deep," Arthur says. "We are down farther than one might imagine." His eyes darken. "And much too dangerous. There are far more dangerous things than the king's men in these woods. You could not travel alone."

The children shiver, as if the same breath of ice has crossed their chests. They know the stories of these woods. They know of the boy the fairies stole once upon a time, who never returned, and the girl and her father, who disappeared in their time. They know of the goblins that turn a child into a slave. They know of the animal creatures that walk on two legs and speak with human voices.

And perhaps it is the great tension in this tomb that cracks Maude, for she buries her face in her hands and cries out, "What will we do?"

They have, perhaps, lived here too long, without venturing into the light of day, but for a simple gathering of vegetables Arthur did every eve. They are, perhaps, too trapped, too exhausted, too hollow of hope.

No one has magic strong enough to get them out of this, is what they are all thinking. No one can save them. No way out.

But there is a girl, slumped in a chair, no longer wrapped in Maude's arms, thinking. Solving. Planning.

Might she be the very one to save them?

Yes. Perhaps she will. But first, let us turn our attention to the castle, where there is some long-awaited news.

Were we to follow the very man who lucked upon a tiny

shoe, we might see him racing out of the woods and into the camp, still spread on the castle lawn. We might, perhaps, see his fellow soldiers turning to look at him, for it is with great shouting and clamoring that this soldier calls for his captain. We might see Captain Sir Greyson standing before the man, looking for all the world as though a soldier of his has gone mad, and then we might see the soldier drop a tiny shoe in the palm of his captain's hand, after which the captain might lean close for inspection and then, in a great shouting of his own, move toward the castle steps.

The soldiers, you see, have waited and waited and waited for news such as this, though one might wonder what it is a shoe might tell them. But they are ready to go home, you see, and so the smallest evidence that a foot has tread through the wood brings them one step closer to returning home.

Sir Greyson bursts into the Great Hall, the shoe in his hand. He clenches his fist around it, to ensure it is still there. "Your majesty," he says. "Your majesty!"

His voice is triumphant, hardly able to contain the excitement that takes his legs and shakes them until they nearly buckle beneath him. For so long they have looked. For so long they have found nothing. And then, today, a shoe. A tiny shoe, to be sure, but a shoe all the same.

Sir Greyson is a smart man. He is not under any illusion that this shoe holds within it the power to send them all home, but hope, as we have agreed, is quite a strange phenomenon. He is already imagining a dinner at home with his mother tonight, if she lives still. He does not consider that this shoe might belong to any being other than one of the missing children. He does not consider that it was a shoe lost in flight, that the children are miles away by now. He does not consider that it means absolutely nothing.

We know it means something, but what is this shoe to the objectively inclined? There is no portal attached any longer. One cannot see an underground house in a tiny shoe.

Perhaps the shoe will lead to something else. This is what bursts our captain through the doors of the throne room.

Prince Virgil sits in a chair beside his father. Sir Greyson has never seen this chair before, nor does he recognize it. But he is too intent on his news to do anything more but notice it. King Willis is eating, as is most often the case, from a plate piled with sweet rolls that his page holds in two hands.

"May I approach the throne, sire?" Sir Greyson says.

King Willis does not speak, for once, with the sweet rolls in his mouth but merely inclines his head in the universal sign for "yes" when one is indisposed to say it with a word. Sir Greyson takes the steps two at a time, which puts him before the king in three steps (for the mathematically challenged, Sir Greyson covers six steps in total). He holds out his hand. The king and the prince stare at his palm.

"Well, what is it?" King Willis says.

Sir Greyson holds it closer to his king, but the king does not have the eyesight he once did as a boy. He squints but cannot make anything out. It is a very small shoe.

Prince Virgil, however, sees the shoe quite clearly. It is not one he recognizes. "A tiny shoe?" he says. "Whatever could that mean? It is much too small for the children we seek."

In his father's presence, Prince Virgil does not consider what might happen to the children the king pursues, though they were once his friends. The very boy King Willis seeks most was Prince Virgil's best friend, but Prince Virgil, under his father's influence and the mysterious hold of the royal throne (we shall come to this at a later time, dear reader. Do not worry.), cares nothing for details such as these. When he is alone in his bedchamber or with his mother, the guilt steals over him, for he is the reason his father pursues his friends. He is the one, after all, who led his father to Theo. He is the one who told the secret of his friend's magic. He is the one who set it all in motion.

But in the throne room, Prince Virgil is merely a prince, nothing more. He is not a friend. He is not a boy who once loved a handful of village children. He is not who he was. And because Prince Virgil has taken to spending more and more time with his father and the king's golden throne, he is losing more and more of who he was. This is the fate of those who keep foolish company, though one cannot blame our prince for spending time with his father. Is it Prince Virgil's fault that his father is more fool than wise man? A boy cannot simply forget his father.

King Willis stands from his throne, though it is growing more and more difficult for him to do every day. "A shoe," he says. "A tiny shoe." He makes a sound, as if he is pondering, too, the question of his son.

"We came upon it in the Weeping Woods," Sir Greyson says. "One of my men discovered it."

"But what does a tiny shoe have to tell us about anything?" Prince Virgil says.

Sir Greyson looks at his prince, then back at his king. "It is the first sign of any life we have found."

"But it could belong to anything," Prince Virgil says. "There are fairies who wear shoes, are there not?"

Sir Greyson shakes his head. It is, to be sure, a foolish question. Fairies, of course, do not wear shoes. But Sir Greyson is a kind man. He does not answer his prince as if he is merely a child. "No, sire," he says, for Prince Virgil will one day be his king. "Fairies are not known to bother with shoes." He clears his throat. "There was a boy."

"A boy?" King Willis says. His eyebrows draw low over his eyes.

"A tiny boy," Sir Greyson says. Even now, he does not like disclosing the news, though moments ago he felt great relief at having found anything, for he, like his men, is ready to return to his home. Desperation, you see, makes a man forget his reason. And now that Sir Greyson stands before his prince and his king, he remembers the plans King Willis has for the children once they are found, and he hopes, in his heart, that they have fled to a place where his men will never find them, that they are, somehow, safe. Yet, if they are, his men will be ordered to continue searching.

How does a man walk himself out of such a conundrum?

Sir Greyson looks at the shoe. He can do nothing about the shoe now. He can do nothing about the words he has already spoken. He must say more.

"A boy in the village," Sir Greyson says. "A boy as small as a thumb."

The king tilts his head. "And this is his shoe?"

"There is no way of knowing for sure, sire," Sir Greyson says. "But I suspect so." He stares at the shoe in his palm.

"And what, pray tell, do you think it means?" King Willis says.

Sir Greyson feels the cloud settle on him. Guilt. Hope. Fear.

All of those battling in a storm of thunder and lightning, in the places one cannot see. His mother. The children. His men. Their families. What did they have to return to without their children? What would his mother do without him? What is a man to do?

"They were in the forest," Sir Greyson says, for he knows that even though many of his men have lost their children, they have not lost their wives.

How is it, you ask, that men would follow the orders of a king who has stolen their children from their homes and dimmed the light of the world? It is a quite understandable question. The king, you see, holds all the power in a kingdom like Fairendale. He controls the seeds the people receive for growing vegetables. He controls the flock of sheep that Hazel, if you remember, set free in the Weeping Woods. (We are not sure where the sheep ended up. Perhaps they returned home. Perhaps they were stolen by fairies, taken to the land that does not grow old for the amusement of the Lost Boys and Girls. They are not so important to our story just yet, so we will leave them wherever they may be.) He controls the fire, the provisions, the flow of medicine. He controls everything, except for the rising and the setting of the sun. And why, you ask, do they not leave the kingdom of Fairendale? Well, reader, is it so easy to leave your home? It is all the people have ever known. And there is hope, again. Hope does not let one give up so easily. And no matter how wretched life gets, the people of Fairendale hope. They hope that one day they will have a better kingdom. They hope that one day another king, a kinder king, will sit the throne. They hope that their hopes will come to pass.

And so the men in Sir Greyson's army remain. They see their provisions sent to their wives and mothers. They try to forget the village that holds no laughter. They try to do their duty and carry on.

"They were in the forest," King Willis says. "And where are they now?"

Sir Greyson swallows. He does not know. His men do not know. But he does not confess his not-knowing to the king. "We will find them," he says instead. "Here is our first clue." He holds the shoe up so the king can see it again. King Willis squints, but as far as his eyesight is concerned, there is nothing in Sir Greyson's hand.

Prince Virgil, however, feels another hope, a darker hope, take root.

Perhaps they will be found. Perhaps his throne will be secured, without the gift of magic. Perhaps he will rule the land after all.

You must understand, reader. Prince Virgil, though once a kind boy, has listened, day after day, to the stories of his father, stories of grandeur and fame, and once dreams of grandeur and fame crawl inside a heart, a man (or woman or boy or girl) will do anything to see them come to pass. Everyone wants to be a part of history. Prince Virgil will be among the names of the Fairendale kings, a most revered calling. He will be feared and respected and, mostly, remembered. He does not know that one can be remembered, too, for the evil one brought to the world, and this is not a fame most would want.

Some, alas, will take fame in whatever package it comes. Prince Virgil is not so far gone as this, but he is coming closer every day, for every hour he spends sitting on his father's throne, though King Willis does not permit it often just yet, is another hour that the light and the dark in Prince Virgil's heart battles.

"Go, then," King Willis says. "Find them." He looks at his son, his lips pulled into a grin. "And when you do, bring them to me."

"Yes, sire," Sir Greyson says. He clutches the shoe in his palm, turns on his heel and strides toward the double doors at the back of the room. His men wait just outside the castle for new orders.

And perhaps the sound of the doors swinging open and clanking closed pulls our prince from the enchantment of this room, this throne, this king, for it is when Sir Greyson has disappeared that Prince Virgil feels the sudden twisting of his stomach.

King Willis is looking at his son. "A feast to celebrate," the king says. "They shall be found. As we knew they would."

Prince Virgil, truth be told, does not feel much like eating. He does not feel much like anything but following on the heels of soldiers who will search the forest once again. He would like to warn the children. He would like to bid them run. He does, after all, still love three of them. Are they alive? Are they safe?

Perhaps he might sneak out of the castle tonight and warn them. Would he be brave enough to venture into the forest?

No, of course not. He has heard the stories. The fairies. The goblins. The shape shifters. There are too many dangers. His friends, if they are in the forest, will not be there for long.

But what if the men find his friends? What if they bring them to his father? What if they die?

Do you see, dear reader, what goes on in the heart of our prince? It is not so very easy to be a prince. It is not so very easy to feel the pull of fame and the love of three people. It is not so very easy to choose between power and love.

"It is only a matter of time," King Willis says. He pats his son, but Prince Virgil does not look at his father's face, for the spell, for now, has been broken. "They will pay."

"Yes," Prince Virgil says. "They will pay." He does not mean the words, of course. For in his heart, he whispers his treason. *Do not let them have Theo or Mercy or Hazel.*

Love, you see, is a powerful thing.

Beneath the ground, in their home with dirt walls and floor and wooden furniture made by the deft hands of Arthur, the children do not know whether it is day or night. They have felt the vibrations of horses and men above ground, and they find themselves inclined to fall asleep to the gentle rhythm. It is not time for sleeping, though dusk is near, but the children have nothing better to do. They eat what little food is left, and then they take to their beds, trying not to think about their great thirst that will widen in the coming hours. Arthur and Maude hole up in their own bedroom. Hazel follows Mercy to the one they share, the other girls retiring to their own. Bunks fold into the earth in a quite remarkable way. One has only to touch a staff to the ground, and out the beds come. Hazel and Mercy sit on Hazel's perfectly made bed. They do not speak for a time. Mercy fingers the blanket that wrinkles where they sit. Hazel's bed looks much different than her own, for Mercy could never see the point of making a bed she would sleep in again.

There is so much to be said between the two friends, but they do not quite know how to say it.

Hazel, who keeps a rigid back most of the time, slumps on the bed. "I do not know what we will do," she whispers, as if she wants no one else to hear her, though the other girls are tucked away in their own rooms. "I do not know how we will survive."

Mercy takes her friend's hand. "We will survive," she says. "We did not come so far to give up so easily."

"But we have no more food," Hazel says. "We have no water." She looks at her friend, as if afraid of the words she has just said. "I am sorry. I do not mean it is your fault."

Mercy dips her head. "We are all doing what we can," she says. "It is not easy with our hunger."

"No," Hazel says. "We thought we were hungry in the village." Her voice catches at the end of it, for Hazel loved her village home and misses it now. She misses, too, the sheep she used to lead, every morning and afternoon, to the freshwater cove for a drink and then back to their grazing fields. She even misses the taunts of the mermaids.

Mercy puts an arm around Hazel's shoulders. Hazel leans on her friend.

"I miss Theo," Hazel says.

Mercy nods against the top of her head. "Me too," she says.

They both wonder the same questions, but they do not dare wonder aloud. Is he still alive? Has he been captured? Will he find safety?

"I know he is alive," Hazel says into the silent chasm. "I would feel it if he was not." In truth, Hazel has grown weaker and weaker every day. She fears it is because her twin grows weaker and weaker every day. She hopes it is merely the hunger. But she has little magic left, if any. It is known that a twin dying strips the magic from the remaining twin. Hazel looks at her staff, resting in the corner with Mercy's. She longs to try. To know. But she does not dare.

"No," Mercy says, as if she knows precisely what it is her friend is thinking. "You must not try. You must not waste what little magic remains."

"But what if there is none left?" Hazel says. She feels the fear burning her eyes. She blinks them.

"There is," Mercy says.

"But we do not know for sure," Hazel says.

"We must trust," Mercy says. "And we must rest."

Mercy climbs to her bed above Hazel's, and the girls lie in their separate places, joined by the minds that do not give in so easily to sleep.

We must rest so we can die, Hazel thinks.

It may work, Mercy thinks.

For Mercy, you see, has a plan.

Across the dirt hall, Arthur and Maude sit on their bed in much the same way Mercy and Hazel did. They sit close, their shoulders touching. Maude slumps. Arthur straightens. They think and do not speak, until Arthur says, "I am sorry."

Arthur, you see, feels as if this burying, this trap beneath the ground, is his fault. It was, after all, his idea to create an underground portal, held in place by a tiny shoe. Perhaps he should have chosen something more permanent. A boulder. A tree. A cave. But a tiny shoe. What are the odds that someone would find a tiny shoe? What are the odds that it would be disturbed from its place, deep in the woods? The king's men must be growing desperate. He should have known.

And now they are trapped, unable to escape. They have eaten their last bowl of carrot soup, for there are no more carrots, and there is no more water. What will they do? How will they survive? Magic has its limits. It cannot keep them alive.

"Oh, Arthur," Maude says. She lays her head on his shoulder, as if they are the very picture of Hazel and Mercy, adults where children sat moments ago. Arthur strokes her hair. He ponders in silence. Maude nearly falls asleep, she is so exhausted. Fear, you see, does different things to different people.

Arthur listens to his wife's gentle breathing. He moves his

arm around her shoulder so that she falls against him. She is warm and beautiful, as she was all those years ago. He kisses the top of their head. They will die. There is no hope. There is no way out of this trap beneath the earth. And what strikes the most fear in the heart of a man like Arthur is that it will not be a quick and easy death. It will be a slow one. A torturous one. Perhaps it would have been better to let the king's men catch the children in the very beginning. Perhaps he should have known they could not stay here forever. Perhaps he should not have ventured back into the lands of his youth.

"Okay, then," Arthur says. Maude startles awake. "Sorry to wake you."

"Okay then?" Maude says, her face brightening with hope, as if, perhaps, Arthur's sudden words mean he has thought of a way out of death.

He shakes his head. He has only, you see, come to terms with dying. He turns to his wife and takes both of her hands in his. "It will not be an easy death," he says.

"No," Maude says.

"We will have to help the children," Arthur says.

"Yes," Maude says. Tears stream down her face. Arthur folds her in his arms.

"I am sorry, love," he says. "I am sorry I failed you."

"You did not fail us," Maude says. "How could we have

known what would happen?"

"It is an underground home," Arthur says. "It is a portal. There are always dangers."

"You kept us alive," Maude says. Her voice is muffled against his chest. "For the time it mattered. And Theo…"

She does not finish her thought, but Arthur knows what she intended to say. Theo might yet be alive. And that matters for something as well, though it makes their dying that much more difficult. His son, alone. Where is he? Why had he run the other way, when the plan had been the woods? They might have used his magic, and Hazel's, too.

Neither of them speaks for a time. And then Maude says, "Is there not something we can do, Arthur? Anything? Some little bit of magic left?"

Arthur shakes his head. "The children are too weak," he says. "The magic would be more powerful than they are." Everyone knows what happens when a magician cannot control his power. The magic will take over, turning good intentions to bad. Magic, you see, does not like its natural hierarchy. Magicians have always been stronger than magic. And so magic will take control wherever it might, which makes it quite dangerous for a magician to practice when he is already weak.

"What about Hazel?" Maude says. "Perhaps she has a bit left. She has not used any magic since we left the village."

"She has been without Theo for far too long," Arthur says. "Asking her to use what might be left would risk the loss of her magic forever."

Maude knows this, of course. But she is thinking of the children. She is wondering if Hazel would do this for the children. "Is not life more important than magic?" Maude whispers. "Can one not live without magic?"

Arthur lets out a long breath. "Of course," he says. "But then what?" He looks toward the ceiling. Maude pulls away.

"Then we escape," she says.

"What is waiting in the woods?" Arthur says. "We do not know if it is night or day."

"It matters not," Maude says. "What is out there is nothing to what it is in here, what we face when the children wake from their sleep. Why not give them this hope? At least we will have tried."

"The king's men wait in the woods," Arthur says.

"We will run," Maude says. "As we did before."

"We will run forever," Arthur says. "They will never stop their pursuit."

"I will run forever," she says. "The children will run forever. To stay alive."

Arthur shakes his head, but, in the end, he knows his wife is right. They will have to ask their daughter to use her magic. It is the only thing left.

And then they will have to risk whatever waits for them in the Weeping Woods.

The shadows stretch long and narrow in the secret shelter beneath the village fountain. There is a woman here, a woman of bright green eyes and flame-colored hair, who looks like one of the children in our story.

She has, in fact, lost a child in this story.

And so she is desperate, as any mother would be, to save the children, for she loves her daughter with a great, unceasing love. She misses her daughter's bright green eyes and flame-colored hair. She misses the magic her daughter made in their cottage, turning azaleas to roses, mending old shoes, making a blanket from a scrap of cloth to replace the one with holes in it. She had this gift once upon a time, though she never learned to tame it as her daughter had. There had not been an Arthur in the village when she was a girl.

There are other people who gather in this room. There are men who have lost sons and grandmothers who have lost grandchildren and mothers, like her, who have lost their daughters. They all want the same thing: the children returned.

The children safe. The children back in their homes, back in the streets, back in a laughter-filled world.

"Where are they?" a man in the corner says. He has a gruff face, a gruff voice, a gruff appearance with his furry chin and wrinkled red tunic and brown breeches of varying length on each leg. The green belt tied about his waist is too loose, for the people of Fairendale do not fare well in these days after the children's disappearance. There is no reason to eat, most of the time. Though when a body is hungry enough, it will eat. This man has lost his twin boys and an older son. He does not understand why his boys would be in danger at all, for they do not seek a throne. They do not have what it takes to rule a kingdom, for they were not born with magic. They are simply boys. Missing boys. Loved boys. Cora knows this man to be Garron, the village gardener.

"I do not know where the children are," says the woman with flaming hair. "The dungeon, we hope."

The people murmur. If one were standing in this candlelit room, one might hear words like, "The dungeon?" and "That is what we hope?" and "Surely not."

"Do you think they are safe?" a woman says. Her eyes are red-rimmed, as if she has been crying. Many of the mothers, you see, have been crying since the day they lost their children. A mother, though not always grateful, perhaps, for the untidiness children bring to a home, always loves her children. It is, in fact, love that has brought them all here, though they wanted nothing more than to remain in their beds and wither away, as it seems the land of Fairendale has begun to do.

"No," Cora says, though she would like nothing more than to say otherwise. "I do not think any children are safe in the kingdom now."

"What will we do?" another woman calls out. Cora does not know these village people all that well, for she never had much need to know them. Her daughter studied magic with Arthur and Maude. She knows the baker, the shoemaker, the tailor, the book binder, the gardener. Only the ones she needs to know. She is accustomed to living a somewhat lonely life, for she was always different from the rest of them. But they need a leader, and a leader they shall have.

"We will go to war," another man shouts, from the middle of the hunched crowd. The other villagers murmur their approval.

Cora knows that the people are untrained for something as violent as war. She has other plans, plans that will involve moving silently, bleeding the castle a day at a time. So she waits until the room has quieted once more, until the candles have settled into a straight-line flicker, rather than a reaching one.

"No," Cora says. "Not yet. Now is the time for planning. For building. For gathering strength and numbers."

The people look at one another. They are gaunt and pale, with purple circles painting the undersides of their eyes. They do, in fact, look worse for wear, as they say. They look as if they may be dying, slowly, though if one were to look with eyes that could truly see, one would not see Death lurking in the shadows of Fairendale any longer. Death is satisfied, for now, though there is no knowing when his hunger will return.

Death, you see, has moved on to stand guard at another place, but we are getting ahead of ourselves.

"We must move before it is too late," says a ragged man with black eyes. "Before the children are lost."

"The children are already lost," Cora says. "We shall find them again, bring them back to our homes, but our plans will take time."

"Plans?" a woman says. A hooded cloak covers her body, bright red. It does not seem to fit, as if, perhaps, it belongs, instead, to a child. Might this woman have a missing child who used to wear this cloak? Why, yes. This woman is wearing her daughter's cloak, and it is a tragic sight.

"Who has made plans?" the woman says.

"I have," Cora says, and she holds a roll of parchment tied with a string so that all the people can see it. "If we are to defeat King Willis, we must have a plan." She unties the string and rolls the parchment out on a nearby table. The people huddle around her, though not everyone can see, for it is a small table, and there are more people than Cora might have expected. This will be good for her plan.

"What we must first do," Cora says, "is return to our duties in the village." She points to the baker. "You, Bertie, must bake bread." She points to the village gardener. "And you, Garron, must tend to the vegetables." She looks around at the people, meeting as many eyes as she can. "We must eat to gain our strength. We must survive."

"But without the children…" a woman from the back says. She is wrinkled and slumped. This woman, you see, had twelve children, and they have all gone missing, except for the oldest one, who is not much of a boy any longer. He remains at the castle, undiscovered. He brings her what he can, but it is not so often as it once was.

"Yes, without the children," Cora says. "Without the children, our work will be harder. But we must help one another. We must share generously with our fellow villagers."

Perhaps Cora knows what words such as these might do for the people of Fairendale. Perhaps she has no idea. It matters not. When they hear the words, it is with a sense of community, a sense of brotherly and sisterly affection, a sense of family. While it is true that Fairendale, in the days before the roundup, boasted of good relationships, in the days after, the people have taken to their beds and hardly see one another. They hardly remember their fellow villagers' names. They hardly know how to live.

It is with a gratefulness of greater depth than words can express that the people turn their faces back to their leader, this woman with scarlet hair and white skin and eyes that hold them fast in the waters of peace and courage and, mostly, hope.

Cora directs them to the plans laid out on parchment—a strengthening time, a stealing time, a training time, and, when all the pieces have fallen into place, an attacking time.

"There is a time," Cora says, ending her speech, "for everything."

The people are silent for some moments, hardly daring to breathe. They do not know if they can do what is asked of them to do. Waiting for so many days? How is it possible to go about life as if nothing has changed, when the streets and their homes do not vibrate with the laughter and presence of their children? How can they bear to tend their gardens and their bakeries and their shoe-making shops, all the pieces of village life, without the children watching and learning and, as they can, helping? How is it that they might do nothing, absolutely nothing, to save their children when they do not yet know where their children sleep or if they live or whether they are forever lost? Is it not dire to immediately begin the search for their children?

"Will it work?" a woman close to Cora whispers. Cora knows her to be the baker's wife. "Will your plan work?"

"One can never know whether a plan will work in its entirety," Cora says. "One must simply try. And hope. And, perhaps, try again."

The villagers, of course, know this. They have lived more than enough years to have learned about trying and failing and trying again, and yet it is astounding what one can forget in the grip of tragedy. This is a tragedy of the highest order for the people of Fairendale, I am sure we can all agree.

Bertie's bald head glows in the candlelight. He nods it. "Yes," he says. "We must try."

"We must plan for food," Cora says, nodding toward him.

"I will need wheat," he says.

"Perhaps the wheat is not so very badly ruined," says Garron, the gruff man in a red tunic. He would do anything to save his three boys. "It is a hearty strain."

"We will harvest at first light," Cora says. "Whatever we can. We will all work together."

The people murmur around them.

"Garron, you will lead us in mending the gardens," Cora says. "With our help, perhaps it can be nurtured back to its former abundance."

"It has been many days," Garron says. "The wheat might be

saved, but the rest, I fear, might be lost. And without new seeds from the castle…" He does not go on.

Cora tries not to think what that might mean. The people could not survive on just wheat. "We will do what we can," she says.

"And if your plan does not work?" says the woman with twelve children. She has watery blue eyes and a sagging chin.

"Then we will plan again," Cora says.

"We will not give up?" says the woman in a child's red cloak.

"No," Cora says. "We will not rest until our children are returned to us."

At this, the villagers nod their heads. Yes. They will fight for their children until their children return home. This is, after all, what parents do.

The room grows quiet again. Someone sniffs in the back.

"We will meet at the gardens at first light," Cora says.

The people nod.

"You must file out one by one," Cora says. "In case there are watching eyes."

There are no watching eyes, of course, for the kingdom is much too concerned with the shoe that was found in the forest. But it is never a bad idea to exercise caution in the most dangerous of situations.

Cora is the last one in the room. She looks over her plans,

wavering in the candlelight, and then she rolls up the parchment, ties the string around it and slips out of the underground meeting place. The lights in the village homes flicker out, one by one, until the whole world goes dark.

Should the townspeople have looked, on stepping out of their secret meeting place, toward the dark wood, and should they have extraordinary night vision, they might have seen a small boy, standing at the edge of the forest. They might have seen him lift his head back to stare at the moon, a small sliver in the sky, almost not there at all, which, of course, makes the night darker than it would be were the moon full and white. They might have seen him take one small step forward and then stop. Another step forward and another stop. Another step, but this one back.

Do you see him? He is, perhaps, slightly hard to see, for he is dressed in a black robe, the robe his mother ordered specially when one was needed for a special princely presentation when he was a boy of six. So it is a bit tight and a bit more short. His breeches are made of the finest cloth, though on a black night like this, one cannot tell. His boots, laced up to the calf, are black as well, so he appears, you see, invisible. Upon leaving the castle, he thought this black night would serve him well, but as he stands before the woods he has never entered but has heard about in fearful tales, he does not so much like the small moon and its not-shining.

Prince Virgil is faced with the most complicated of decisions. Should he enter, for the sake of finding his friends? Should he risk his life and the ire of the fairies, who are known to take anyone who wanders the woods when the sun has vanished, with his trespassing, though he does not know if his friends wait inside? Should he return back home, back to his warm bed, back to the fire that waits to not only warm but also to light his chambers?

He does not feel like a brave boy. A brave boy would have no trouble stepping within the cover of trees. But Prince Virgil, a very decidedly not-brave boy, waits. Stares. Feels a heart flipping wildly in his chest.

And then, alas, a creature from within the dark woods, growls. Another creature howls. And yet another hoots, and as Prince Virgil stares, the dark forest fills with eyes. And so he turns. He flees. He leaves his friends to their fate, which is, perhaps, as it should be.

Prince Virgil runs for his very life, for he does not know whether the creatures within the wood follow him. He does not look back. He stumbles on the path, numerous times, but then he sees the bridge, and he has only to cross it to be safe from whatever may have followed him. He has only to make it to that bridge, and whatever evil pursues him will not cross. He knows this from stories his mother used to tell him as a young boy. So though he is tired, for he runs harder than he has ever run before, Prince Virgil summons enough energy to run even harder. Fear, as it happens, is an excellent motivator.

Somewhere above our prince a bird watches, flying along with him, its wings keeping time with the steps of our prince, who appears, at a distance, like an oversized bird himself, for his black cape flaps behind him like great, magnificent wings.

Prince Virgil is terrified of birds. It was a bird, you see, who tore out the eyes of his grandfather and hastened the former king's death. Might this bird be the very one that visited his grandfather on a night much like this one? Might this bird be a foe? Might this bird be flying for blood?

Fortunately, our prince does not see this bird. Fortunately, it is too high in the black sky. Fortunately, it does not speak its ominous cry.

So it is a mystery what trips up Prince Virgil's steps on the bridge. Is it a rock? A hand? Another bird, waiting?

What is happening now, dear reader? Could that be Prince Virgil's head, careening toward stone? Could that be his body spread flat on the ground, as if he has spent every ounce of his being on this terrified run? Could that be a bird, perched on his back, while his cheek presses stone?

Why, yes. Yes it is.

Fortune

Greyson had always been a merry boy, from the time he was born. He was a child who helped wherever he might, cooking with his mother in the kitchen or running to fetch his father on the nights he got caught in conversation with the other men in the village and supper sat on the table, growing cold. Greyson loved running through the streets and watching the girls do their magic and seeing the blacksmith and the baker and the shoemaker work. He especially liked watching the bookmaker. Though his home did not have many books, Greyson loved stories and so watching stories be made, bound together as a book, was of great entertainment.

Because he was an only child, Greyson had to help both his father and his mother, though his father was a soldier and only needed his sword shined every now and again. Sometimes he would try on his father's armor, and his father would laugh heartily at the tiny bit of boy and the large bit of steel.

Every evening Greyson and his parents would sit around the fireside while his mother told stories of distant lands and magic and the mermaids of the Violet Sea. He always tried to spy the mermaid's tail at the very moment the sky flashed golden, for he was one who believed in the fortune of such a sight at such a time. Alas, he never did see it. And this is why Greyson believed that he, perhaps, was not one of those that fortune smiles upon, for not only had he never seen a mermaid's tale at sunset, but he was also always skinning his knees and catching colds and burning supper. His parents shook their heads and laughed, ruffling his sandy hair and calling him their clumsy lad. He did not think this was funny, of course, as I am sure no child would, but he tried not to let it bother him much. In the space between stories and sleep, his mother whispered that one day he would outgrow it. And he believed her.

He was a friend of all, calling the adults by name, greeting respectfully, patting the younger children on their heads. The children would always come running when Greyson emerged into the streets, for he kept his pockets full of the special candies his father brought home from his travels. His father was captain of the king's guard, and in those days there were many travels, for the kingdom of Fairendale was still repairing the damage done by the Great Battle, though it had been nearly eighty-three years since King Sebastien marched the men of all the lands toward death. All those men of King Sebastien's were mysteriously lost, and the other kingdoms were not so happy to have given up their most strapping young men. Greyson's father was a peacemaker, though, and this is what kept the other lands from storming Fairendale's castle. He brought with him seeds from the flowers of Fairendale, for its beauty was widely told and celebrated.

Because of his father's position within the palace, Greyson and his family were well cared for. They had more than enough food and clothes and medicine. Greyson tried to share whenever he could, though he had heard stories of the prince who had been banished from the castle for doing just that. Greyson thought it a very sad story and asked that his father never tell it again, and his father never had. Even so, Greyson could not forget it.

In the kingdom of Fairendale, as it existed when Greyson was a boy, a person could be punished for sharing what excess he had. So Greyson grew discreet about it. The children, then, would gather round him, and he would wave them away, and just before their going, he would slip the leader, who would share with the rest, a bag of candy or some cookies his mother had made or one of the baker's famous bon bons. They would walk away with it hidden in their tunic, and he knew they would savor it later.

Most days, when Greyson finished his household chores, he would wander the streets in search of his father and find him talking with the men of the village in the watering hole, which served some kind of drink that smelled sour and tasted even worse. Greyson's father usually had a tall glass of it in front of him. He dressed always in black, a cape gathered round his shoulders. It was not often that Greyson saw his father in his armor.

There Greyson would sit, listening to his father and the men of Fairendale tell the kingdom's stories.

Greyson was not born the day King Sebastien moved into town, but most of the stories told by the villagers were about The Good King Brendon, the king Sebastien had defeated when he invaded the land, the king the people of Fairendale had all loved dearly. In fact, one could never hear The Good King Brendon's name without "The Good" preceding it. So King Brendon became The Good King Brendon in all the history stories. They were stories told throughout the generations, since none of those who lived at this time in our story had been alive when The Good King Brendon ruled the throne. He was known as the wisest and kindest and bravest of all kings. And though the people told these stories of the good king for the hope they held, they did not look so hopeful at the end of them, only despondent. This made Greyson sad. So he and his father would walk home sad, and his mother would say, "Why are my men so sad?" and she would ruffle their hair and move into the kitchen, where she had baked some kind of surprise while they were out telling and listening to stories. They would sit around the table eating apple pie or cinnamon cookies or cream puffs, and Greyson would think that even though he had never seen a mermaid's tail at sunset, he was the most fortunate person in all the world.

Until the day it all changed.

Gone

It is now early morning, though the children and Arthur and Maude have no way of knowing this. They gather around a breakfast table, for they do not know the hour or the day, only that their bellies rumble from hunger. They know, simply, that they have woken, that this is, perhaps, the last day they will live, for water has not been summoned by Mercy since their sleeping. It appears as though Mercy's powers are waning ever more. But perhaps everything is not as it appears.

The children, in truth, did not sleep well in the night. Neither did Arthur or Maude. It seems that knowing one will wake to a day that could be one's very last does not make it easy to sleep. The children feel they should have celebrated, perhaps, for a last night alive is a thing to celebrate, is it not?

But they have drawn together at a breakfast table that must be larger than any we have ever seen, for there are twenty-six of them seated around it. They do not speak, nor do they look at one another. The mood, as it happens, is quite sullen.

The curve of Maude's back straightens slightly. "Shall we turn the last of our possessions into bread?" she says. She knows they will no longer need what few possessions they have, particularly if this is their last day living.

Arthur nods. And then, poor man, his face crumbles, the stubbly growth on his cheeks and chin shaking, and he says, "I am sorry children. I am sorry there was not another way."

Hazel's cheeks, despite the hunger, have remained rosy red. She feels this loss the most, perhaps, for if her brother were here, if he had come with them, they might have had enough magic left to flee once more. But her magic is little more than a child's tricks now. She tried, this morning, one last time, and she got nothing for her efforts. Alas, she is too hungry to be of much use, and, what is more, her magic is significantly weakened without her brother's. She would be at a disadvantage even if she had a full belly.

Where is her brother? Has magic saved him? Is he on his way to find her? Theo always had the greatest plans, more like Arthur than Maude. Hazel wishes, for the thousandth time, that her brother had simply followed her into the woods, instead of trying to save a handful of children. Look how many would perish at his choice.

This is how sadness turns to anger, you see. Hazel wishes her brother were here for the simple fact that she loves him. But brooding on his missing piece sets her to pondering the circumstances that led to his disappearance. Theo saw some children in need, and, rather than moving toward the woods where they had a hope of safety and togetherness, he moved toward the younger children. Heroic, but foolish. And now they will all perish.

A couple of the children sniffle, though no one speaks still.

Mercy coughs into her hand, as if clearing her throat for something important she has to say. Hazel looks at her friend. Mercy's green eyes are glazed, the way they get when she has done much thinking. Her scarlet hair is not so vibrant as it was before they entered this underground home. Starvation shows in many different places.

"I could do something," Mercy says.

The words startle everyone gathered around the table. Maude is still breaking off tiny chunks of bread, passing it around, for there is not much. But the children do not reach for their pieces. They look, instead, to Mercy.

"What do you mean, you could do something?" Arthur says. He looks at Maude. She shakes her head, as if it say, *It is too dangerous to risk the life of a child*. Though she does not know the plan, she assumes that it is a dangerous one, for the king's men have found their traps, and they have found the portal, so it seems. What plan would not be dangerous?

"I still have a bit of magic left," Mercy says.

"But you could not draw water from the ground," says Ursula, a girl with raven hair.

"I could," Mercy says. "I did not."

"You hid this from us?" says a boy named Chester. His soil-brown eyes narrow. "You would have us die?"

"I would have you live," Mercy says. "Please. Hear me."

The room falls quiet. Arthur is the first to speak. "Very well," he says. "You have a plan."

"I still have magic," she says. "I have saved my magic for this plan."

"What plan?" Arthur says.

"The plan that will save us," Mercy says.

The children look at one another. Hazel looks at her friend. She cannot ignore the fear that settles in her chest.

"Let us hear your plan," Arthur says. He is hopeful, you see. Mercy was his most promising student, before they became trapped underground and the food and water began to disappear. She could do magic Arthur had not seen in years. He had once, very recently, considered approaching her mother for permission to do advanced magic lessons, the first of his pupils to reach such a level.

"I could disappear," Mercy says. She breathes, a soft exhale, as if she is trying to convince herself that this is not so very dangerous after all. "I could reappear."

The children stare at her, their mouths open. No one has touched their bread. Is it hope that draws their mouths open in this way? Or is it fear for their friend?

This is, you see, quite a dangerous spell. When one vanishes into thin air, one never knows whether one will reappear. If one does reappear, one does not know what sort of skin one will wear. Will one be old and bent? Will one be young and vibrant? Will one be human at all?

"I cannot allow it," Arthur says. "It is far too dangerous."

Mercy stands up. She is not typically a child who defies her elders, but she is the best hope they have. She knows this. She will not let their hope pass by without a try.

"There is nothing else we can do," Mercy says.

Arthur and Maude stare at her.

"There is nothing else," she says again. "We will all die." She looks around at the children.

"It is too dangerous," Hazel says. "You cannot. We could all die anyway."

"I am willing to risk my life," Mercy says. She looks as though she is about to cry. Where is their faith in her magic? Where is their permission? Where is their hope? Is it really so very easy to let go of hope?

"There is nothing else," Maude says, and now the children turn to her. Arthur's shoulders slump, for he knows, too, that this is so.

Mercy smiles the smallest smile a person could ever see, just a slight bit of hope gathered in the corners. Maude, you see, is not so easy an ally. "I will disappear," Mercy says. "I will reappear. I will restore the portal with something I carry, something I wear, whatever I may find. And you will all run."

"And you will run," Hazel says, for her friend has not told them all the other part of her plan.

Mercy shakes her head. "No," she says. "I will return to the village to look for Theo. And when I find him, we will come to you. We will find you."

The room grows very quiet. There are so many eyes on her face that Mercy's heats up to a red sort of color, splotchy and uneven.

"You must come with us," Arthur says. "Or we cannot allow it."

"Our only hope is finding Theo," Mercy says. "Finding Theo and bringing him to Hazel. Letting their magic strengthen one another. It is the only way we will escape."

"Perhaps it is not best to escape," Arthur says.

Maude gasps. "Arthur," she says. "What is this?"

"Perhaps it is better to give ourselves up? To fall on the mercy of the king?" Arthur says. His words come out like a question.

"Never," Maude says. "The king has no mercy."

The children look at each other. It is true. There is no mercy in a single bone of the king's body, as far as they know. Not anymore. If there were, the children who do not possess the gift of magic would, today, be safe.

"It is the only way," Mercy says. "This plan."

"But what if it does not work?" Ursula says.

"Then we will at least have tried," Mercy says.

"I cannot," Arthur says, and the tears streak down his face. He pulls Mercy into a tight embrace that dislodges all the emotion she has held in her throat all morning. She, too, has loved this man, this father who is not really her father. He has always protected her, taught her, counseled her in what to do, and now it is she who must save him. Perhaps she will die. But is it not a noble sacrifice to try?

And when they are done with their tearful goodbye, Arthur says, "Very well," and then, again, "very well. You must go." His lips pull tight in a grimace. It is not so very easy to allow a child you love to walk into Death's jaws, though there is a chance that Mercy could survive.

Mercy turns to her best friend. "What if you do not

reappear?" Hazel says. "What if we are trapped down here anyway? What will it have accomplished?"

"I will have done my part," Mercy says.

"But you could do your part pulling water from the ground," Hazel says. Her eyes are red and shining.

"And we would still be trapped," Mercy says. "We would still be starving."

Hazel dips her head, then brings it back up to look at her friend. "How will I know you?"

"I will find you," Mercy says. "Do not worry."

But of course, one will worry when one loves a friend as Hazel loves Mercy.

Mercy hugs the rest of the children and then kisses the cheek of Maude and, once more, hugs Hazel.

"Take care, my friend," Hazel says. "And hasten back."

"I will," Mercy says. She pulls away and looks into Hazel's eyes. "And I will bring with me your brother."

And then, in a single breath, Mercy disappears, and the house beneath the ground grows silent.

King Willis is pacing the throne room, and while he paces he thinks, and while he thinks he talks about what he will do with the missing children when they are, at last, found and returned to the castle.

He will beat them, no, he will let them starve in the dungeons beneath the dungeons, no he will feed them to the creatures of the forest, no, he will tie them up and—

Queen Clarion bursts into the throne room, and though the distance between the door and his throne is wide and vast, it is her voice that disturbs him from his thinking.

"Willis!" she cries. "Willis, you must come at once!"

But the king, self-absorbed man he is, does not notice the terror and panic clutching his wife's words. So she must run the entire length along the blood-red carpet to the foot of the throne. He does not seem to notice her until she says, "It is Virgil."

"What?" he says. "What is it you say, woman?" King Willis, you see, is not so very polite to this woman he claimed to love once.

Queen Clarion bristles at his contempt, but she does not waste words on a matter that must wait for later, for there is a more pressing matter that must be seen to.

"Our son!" she says. "He has disappeared!" The news, even now, even while she has had whole minutes to digest it, is so shocking, it steals her very breath.

The golden chalice in King Willis's hand drops to the floor

in a clanging crash. Garth, the king's page, rushes to clean up the mess of red wine that pools into a stain at the foot of the king.

"What is this?" King Willis says. "What is this you say?"

So the queen repeats this disturbing bit of news. She noticed Prince Virgil missing in the morning, when she knocked on his chambers to see if he would like breakfast. She did not think anything amiss. Her son, after all, sometimes disappears in the early morning hours, for he enjoys walking the grounds, and, before the children disappeared, he often made his way into the village at first light. But she has not found him in the village, nor has she found him on the castle grounds or in the gardens. She realizes now that she did not think to look near the bridge, for her son was terrified of the Violet Sea, even if the bridge crossed only a small freshwater tributary and not the open sea.

When King Willis makes no move and does not speak, Queen Clarion says, "Our son. He is gone."

"Gone?" King Willis says, as though he still does not quite understand. "What do you mean, our son is gone?"

"Disappeared," she says. "He has vanished." Her voice rises a bit, tight and panicked. King Willis shakes his head, as if shaking off a fog.

"Then find him," he says.

"I have been searching," she says. "I have searched all

morning. I do not know where he could be. Perhaps someone…” But you see, dear reader, she cannot say the words. She cannot even think the words.

Perhaps someone has taken him.

“Look harder,” King Willis says, as if he has forgotten that this woman who stands before him is a queen, not a servant. “He must be here somewhere. Search the entire village.”

“But I cannot do it alone,” Queen Clarion says. She wrings her hands. “I need help.” The last word breaks in her mouth, for Queen Clarion is terribly afraid. Afraid that, perhaps, her son entered the woods without a single soul knowing, and now he has disappeared to that land where boys never grow old. Afraid that one of the villagers has taken him so that they may bargain with the king to have their children returned to them. Afraid that he has run away. Afraid that he is in danger. Afraid that she, his mother, will never see him again.

“Well, then, get help,” King Willis says.

“All the men of the guard,” Queen Clarion says, “are in the woods.”

“As they should be,” King Willis says.

He is distracted today, you see. It is not entirely his callous heart that answers so flippantly, so unaffectedly, so harshly. His son has disappeared, and he is not thinking clearly, and the children must be found, and now his son must be found, and what is a king to do?

Queen Clarion takes a deep breath. "We must call them home," she says. "For our son."

"Call them home," King Willis says. "But what about the missing children?"

"Our son has become a missing child," Queen Clarion says. Her voice, this time, wears stone. "Call the king's guard home."

King Willis and Queen Clarion stare at one another for a time. And then King Willis says, "Very well, then. I shall call them home."

What is it, dear reader, that induces our king to change his mind? Perhaps he has seen something in Queen Clarion's eyes. Perhaps he has felt the full loss of a son in these few breaths between Queen Clarion's words and his own. Perhaps there is another reason entirely. It is quite impossible to know.

Queen Clarion follows Garth out to the front steps of the castle and stands on the marble slab that leads to the first of them. Garth looks toward the village, then shifts ever so slightly toward the distant line of forest trees that lie west of the castle and blows a bugle loud enough for all the kingdom to hear.

The people of the village look out their windows. The call

comes loud and clear and long, piercing the gray sky like a gold sword ripping the clouds in two, dividing their hearts in two. Hope. Danger. Which shall it be? They have never heard a sound such as this one, though they have heard of its significance, in the stories told of King Sebastien and his war with their ancestors. Is it a war cry? Is it a call for the people to assemble? Is it a warning of danger? They cannot remember.

Cora, in her home, looks toward the castle, its great gray towers touching the sky, it seems.

"Something has happened," she says, though there is no one in her home to hear it. "Something has happened." And she flies out her door.

She is not the only one. There are others moving from their homes, racing down the road, kicking up red-brown dust, a sight that has not been seen since The Good King Brendon's days on Fairendale's throne, when he opened up the castle grounds for a Year's Last Day feast, in which royal people mingled with common people. The people had loved him for his love, but a king's rule, alas, cannot last forever.

The people fly toward the castle, on their way to see if there are children, long lost, beloved children who will be released.

Or, perhaps, worse.

Sir Greyson, too, hears the call that is intended for him. He knows precisely what it means. He must bring his men back to the castle. But, you see, he does not want to neglect his duties in the woods, either, for he knows that a man like King Willis is not a man always given to reason. King Willis is a man who might one moment call his captain home and, another, flay him for leaving the woods unguarded. And so it is that he divides his men in two, some who will stay, some who will go, and he takes more of the men with him, for he knows the nature of the call. One blow for an announcement of the kingly kind. Two blows for danger. Three blows for dragons of the unfriendly sort.

Sir Greyson waits for a third blow, but there is none. Two blows. Danger.

It is impossible for him to know what sort of danger, for Fairendale could not be under attack, could it? They have peaceful relations with most of the kingdoms. Had King Willis upset that fine balance in his letters?

The captain looks at the gray sky. It is vague, like the call. He has never liked vague.

Perhaps it is merely a simpler kind of danger. Perhaps it is no danger at all, merely a kingly announcement. After all, it has been years upon years since they have used the bugle call. Perhaps the bugler forgot what the calls mean.

He entrusts the woods, this place where a tiny shoe has been found, where his men search, once again, for the missing children, to his second-in-command, Sir Merrick.

"Watch these woods well," Sir Greyson says to Sir Merrick, before taking to his horse and embarking on another flight. He and a bit more than half his men vibrate through the woods, leaving one danger behind and moving, perhaps, toward another.

Journey

It was a bright, sunny afternoon with not a cloud marring the sky, a typical sky of this most beautiful of all kingdoms, when Greyson's father came to him and said, "I must leave on the morrow, at first light."

"But where, Father?" Greyson said, for his father had only just returned from another trip, and it was unusual for him to travel so much this time of year. They were coming up on the Year's Last Day and the new Year's First Day, and though nothing much kind could be said of King Willis, he did always let his men spend those days with their family.

"The king asks that I take some men with me to Ashvale," his father said.

"But for what?" Greyson said. He was a strapping boy of sixteen now, his face mostly smooth lines and patchy stubble. His father put an arm around him, though Greyson stood almost as tall as he did.

"It is a routine peace-keeping trip," his father said, which Greyson knew to be code for "Someone is angry again and I have to fix it." One could not speak so freely in the streets of Fairendale, for there were always ears listening, and one did not know if they were the right ears. The king was said to have a spy, though no one had ever seen him. "Nothing to concern yourself about. I will return before you know it." His father cleared his throat. "We will have dinner early tonight. And then I must rest before the departure." He looked at his son, his eyes flashing with laughter. "Try not to be late."

Greyson, you see, for all the good that was in him, had most always been late for supper. Usually he was about in the streets, talking with the children or with the men, sometimes visiting the widows. Sometimes watching the girls and their magic.

Sometimes watching one girl.

"Yes, sir," Greyson said.

His father ambled away, and there she was, before him. She did not speak, was merely passing in the street, but he could not see anything else but her.

She was the most skilled of all the girls in the village, said to have a great gift of magic that made her fit for a king. Greyson was not king, but she was beautiful, and his eye was caught.

As far as he could see there was only one problem. She was

older than he. No, that was not the problem, of course. The problem was that it was known about the village that she despised men, for she had once been promised to Prince Willis, before he was king, but the arrangement fell through when his brother was banished and there was another girl with stronger magic already living within the castle walls. The girl did not even speak to men any longer. Whatever Greyson tried to do to catch her eye, she would not be moved. But still he tried, and now she was nearing the age when it was said a woman would never marry.

He watched her from the street. Her flaming hair shook about her shoulders. It was long and straight, swinging into her face until she flung it back out. Her grassy eyes met his for a moment, or half of one, and then looked away, as if she did not, in fact, see him standing there at all.

She touched her staff to the ground, and the flower before her dried up.

"Why must you do that?" Greyson said. "Why must you steal its beauty?"

She did not speak to him, as if she had not heard.

She moved toward the water fountain. He followed her. And when she turned, when she hoisted herself up to the lip of the stone, she finally spoke. "You are like a shadow," she said.

His cheeks grew warm. He turned away.

"Do not go just yet," she said. He turned back around. She had never spoken more than five words to him, and that was only moments ago. Her eyes watched him, burned him. She held a flower in her hands. "See. It is better." She held it out to him. "Take it. Please." She leaned against her staff.

He shook his head. His tongue always felt tangled when he was around her. He could find no words now, much less trust them to leave his mouth.

"Have you nothing to say, boy?" she said. The young men in the village whispered that she was cruel. Perhaps he should have left her alone.

"Yes," he said. "Just…" But he could not finish.

She smiled at him as if she knew what he might have said if the words had come more easily. "I am beautiful," she said. "And you. You are besotted." Her eyes grew soft for a moment. She walked closer to him. Her emerald skirt, trimmed with black, bunched around the dirt so he could not see her feet. She was said to walk barefoot, but he could not confirm whether this was true or merely story. She was close enough to touch him now, which she did. She patted the side of his face. "You are too young, boy," she said. She tossed the word "boy" at him. He had nothing else to do but catch it, hold it, wear it. She turned her back. "You are too young to understand."

"I am not," he said, and he sounded every bit of a boy. She

whirled around. "I will be seventeen in a few months."

"And I," she said, "will be nineteen. Do you think a woman of nineteen could love a boy of seventeen? Look at me." She crossed her arms across her chest and looked more beautiful than ever. "I am a woman. You are merely a boy."

And then she danced away on light feet, her staff tapping the ground until she was lost in darkness.

"You are wrong," he said to the empty space that grew between them. And then he returned home, where his mother and father had already begun their supper.

Before retiring to bed, Greyson and his father said their goodbyes. The two men hugged, Greyson's father kissing the top of his head, and as he walked to his room, Greyson tried to ignore the dark feeling spreading in the pit of his stomach.

When he woke, his father was gone.

Bridge

Those underground do not hear the bugle call, for the earth is too thick. But they do feel the shaking of the ground, and then, miraculously, the restoration of the portal. The children cheer. Maude silences them, for something else has caught her keen eye, twirling in from the portal. It is a strip of cloth, a grayish sort of color, with the single word, "Wait" written in black fountain pen, bearing Mercy's handwriting. The children look at each other. No one had a fountain pen, did they?

"Wait," Maude says. "There must be danger. She has seen the danger, and she is ensuring that it does not find us." Maude looks at Arthur. He smiles sadly.

Maude and Arthur know there are dangers in the Weeping Wood that have nothing to do with the king's men. Perhaps Mercy emerged in the dead of night, when creatures roam and stalk. Or perhaps it is the lesser danger—men.

You might wonder, dear reader, why these woods bear the name "Weeping Woods." One would have to read a story called "The Good King's Fall," which the children of Fairendale have been told all their lives, to understand why, but I shall do my best to explain it here. These are the very woods, you see, where King Sebastien's men marched in the Great Battle, the very woods where the dragons of Morad opened their jaws and breathed fire onto the enemy, the very woods where most of the dragons fell. They have long since disappeared, those bodies, though no one knows, exactly, where they went. The woods were practically destroyed in the fire, but when they grew back, they grew darker and more dangerous and crowded with mysteries of which even Arthur and Maude do not know the names. Those creatures come out in the dark of night, the very moment the sun sets. So, you see, it is quite dangerous for a child to walk the woods herself, and it is dangerous for all these children to emerge with Arthur and Maude, if it is, in fact, night. We know it is not, but the ones trapped underground have no way of knowing. And so they wait.

They must not wait very much longer, for then they will not have enough light to flee these woods, and what might happen if they do not find a hiding place come sundown?

Maude looks at Arthur. He looks at her. Neither of them knows quite what to do. They wait.

They wait for hours. They wait for days, for weeks, for months. At least this is what it feels like, locked underground, with nothing to do, with a hunger and a thirst that one can feel in one's head and shoulders and even to the tips of one's feet. They wait until they cannot possibly wait a moment longer.

Were they on our side, dear reader, they would know that they wait precisely a quarter hour. Just long enough for all the king's men to disappear in pursuit of a light, after one of them shouted out, "Magic!" and the rest of them turned to see a shining ball that could very well hold all the missing children inside, for such is the nature of magic. And if Maude and Arthur and the children could have seen this glowing orb, they would have called it green.

The soldiers chased this green object through the woods, jumping to grab it when it seemed reachable, racing farther and farther away from the spot where Maude and Arthur and all the children would emerge into the light of day.

So when they stepped through the portal, not a single man or woman was to be found. Not even Mercy.

Hazel begins to cry.

King Willis waits on the castle steps. The village people

reach him before his royal guard. "My son," he says to them, though they could not possibly empathize with a king who has lost his son, could they, now, dear reader? He has, after all, stolen their children from their homes. "My son is missing!"

And it is true that the villagers know this desperation, this pain that could never be explained, the suffocating panic that clamps a parent heart in a grip much like the one the cobbler must use to mend shoes. Yet before them stands the man who caused it all. Perhaps he deserves this pain. Perhaps knowing it will soften his heart. So the people hope.

And yet King Willis does not make this connection. Queen Clarion, though, is standing beside him, and she cannot look into the faces of the villagers, for fear that she will see the very reflection of her own pain. And then, in a great act of courage, she does look. She is surprised to note, however, that it is not so much pain that twists their faces and shadows their eyes, so much as it is anger. They stare at their king, without saying a word. It is clear that the hatred crackles between them.

"We need your help," King Willis says now. Queen Clarion would not have advised such a foolish request, but the king is not a man who will listen closely to women, though women hold wisdom in as great a supply as any man ever did. "We need your help to find them."

Poor Queen Clarion. She has married a very daft man,

indeed. What sort of person would help their king find his missing son, when that king has taken all their sons and daughters and holds them, still, as his prisoners in the darkest dungeon one could ever see? Certainly none of these people.

The people stare at their king, and their looks grow darker.

"Your children are safe," Queen Clarion calls out.

"Woman!" King Willis says, and he turns to Queen Clarion, raising his hand as if to strike her. Someone in the crowd shouts.

"You are no king," the anonymous voice says. It belongs to a woman. Or, perhaps, a man with a higher-pitched voice. Queen Clarion cannot tell from where it originates. "You are a coward."

King Willis roars toward his people. His face has, in seconds, grown red as the flowers that line the castle steps. "My son is missing!" he says. "Search for him!"

"What about our children?" another voice calls. Deep this time, a man's, surely. Queen Clarion searches the crowd for the owner, but there are too many. King Willis's head whips back and forth, back and forth, back and forth.

"Who said that?" he says, but, of course, the people do not answer. Who would answer an angry king when certain punishment waits for the offender?

"Give us our children," another voice calls out, this one a woman's. Queen Clarion squints. They must be hiding the speakers. "And perhaps we will help you find yours."

"Obey your king!" King Willis shouts, but the people do not move. "Or suffer the consequences of treason!" Still, the people do not move, except to shake their heads in the most imperceptible movement Queen Clarion has ever seen. She feels it more than she sees it, deep in her heart. If there were a way she could change this man, the king. If there were a way she could use her magic.

The people look as if at any moment they will storm the castle stairs, their anger building to a collective fire, and then the sounds of a thousand hoofbeats dance upon the air.

It is the captain. Queen Clarion looks toward the woods. The king's men are coming. The people turn. Sir Greyson pulls up short.

"What is this?" Sir Greyson says. He looks at the people. He looks at his king. "Your highness?"

And the king, you see, is torn right down the middle. Should he command his captain to capture all the people who did not listen to his orders, or should he command his captain to begin the search for his son? Every moment is another moment of danger for his son. And yet if he does nothing about the defiance of his people, what will they do next? He must maintain his power. He must.

In the space between Sir Greyson's question and King

Willis's answer, Queen Clarion's gentle voice says, "Our son. He is missing."

Sir Greyson looks at the people again. "The prince is missing?" he says. There. There is his mother. She is walking. She is here. She is looking at him, meeting his eyes with her wrinkle-rimmed ones. Her face wears something he has never seen before. Shame? Disappointment? Sorrow, perhaps? He is not sure. One could get lost in those wrinkles.

"Find him," the king commands, but Sir Greyson cannot stop looking at his mother. She has become so old. So gray. So wrinkled. When did this happen? While he searched for the children, his mother grew old.

And now he is being asked to search for another child, when he is so close to finding the others?

She does not want him to do it. She would like nothing more than for Sir Greyson to take the people's side. That much is clear in her watery eyes, still fixed upon him. Sir Greyson's mother, you see, does not know why he does what he does. If she did, dear reader, she would urge him to let her die, for she would rather have a son who did what was right than a son who kept her alive.

What will this man of honor do? Will he listen to his mother, to the words she does not speak, or will he listen to his king, to the words that feel heavy and black?

Sir Greyson is so tired of searching. He is so tired of the dilemma. He does not answer his king. He does not answer his mother. What he does, instead, is take off his helmet, trying to speak across mind and space, so that his mother will understand. He has taken vows, you see. Vows he must uphold, vows that require him to do whatever it is his king commands, vows to protect the kingdom. Vows to leave his family behind.

Please understand, Mother, his eyes say.

But his mother only turns away.

"Captain?" the king says, surprised that his captain has not immediately begun his search, since Sir Greyson usually follows his king's orders as soon as they are made. "The prince must be found."

"Yes, sire," Sir Greyson says. "As you command."

And then, as if the world has split open and dissolved into song, a voice pierces the air. All the people turn. Sir Greyson dismounts from his horse. He walks to the bridge, where it seems the sound grows louder. He peers over the edge. A group of mermaids gathers around something. A sack? A body? Perhaps a boy?

Queen Clarion puts her hand to her mouth. Somehow, she is beside Sir Greyson, peering down as well. "My boy," she says.

Is this the price they must pay for all that King Willis has done? Is this what will be taken from them? Her beloved son?

Her boy who used to sit on her lap when she read to him from ancient storybooks?

Why could it not have been his father?

In the crowd, Cora watches her queen. Her heart twists the slightest bit. There was a time, you see, when Cora and the queen were great friends, and a time, soon after, when they became great enemies, and yet now, witnessing the grief that bounds across her old friend's face, Cora cannot help but empathize. She knows how it feels to lose a child. She has, after all, lost her only daughter. The daughter who might have married the prince, reuniting the friends once more. But such happy endings do not always come to pass.

Cora moves closer to the bridge, but she does not dare join her queen.

Sir Greyson bounds down the hill, toward the water beneath the bridge. A boy is cradled in the arms of the mermaids. They look at Sir Greyson as he approaches, hissing and warning him to keep his distance.

"He is not well," they say.

Sir Greyson backs away. Mermaid teeth are said to be sharper than the point of a dagger, and he knows, from the stories, that mermaids do not take kindly to people walking on the land so near their waters, unless, of course, they take an interest in the person. Sir Greyson does not have their interest today, though any other day he might, for Sir Greyson, though many years older than the boy, is a handsome man, with ruddy cheeks, turquoise eyes and hair the color of the dust along the road to the village.

Is the land beneath the bridge the mermaids' terrain? Or does it belong to the king? Sir Greyson does not know for sure. He only knows that he must deliver the prince to his king. He looks up at the bridge. Queen Clarion and King Willis stare down at him. Villagers crowd around the sides. He turns back to the mermaids, who stroke Prince Virgil's curls.

"He is alive?" Sir Greyson says.

"Barely," they say. "He is wounded."

"Where?" he says.

"His head," says a particularly beautiful mermaid. Her crimson hair billows out behind her, the wind shaking it in waves. Sir Greyson pulls his eyes from her face. Mermaids are dangerous creatures to look upon. The stories say they make a man fall in love with them so quickly he loses reason and it becomes easy for her to drag him down into the depths of the water. The mermaids do not always live under this bridge, of course. They come back for entertainment, to watch the people, to sun on the rocks with their tails still touching the salty waters of the Violet Sea.

"I need him," Sir Greyson says. He points toward the prince.

"He is ours now," a black-haired beauty says. Sir Greyson takes a step closer. She bares her teeth, which, just moments ago, stood perfectly white and straight behind a perfectly reddened mouth. Now look at her. Showing her fangs.

But Sir Greyson is a courageous man. That much must be said. "No," he says. "He belongs to the kingdom."

"He fell into our water," the black-haired mermaid says. "He would have drowned without our help."

This puzzles Sir Greyson, for he thought mermaids did not care so much about drowning, if the stories are true. "Why did you spare him?" he says.

"He might be useful later," the red-haired one says.

"But you must release him," Sir Greyson says.

"Not a chance," the red-haired one says. "I have taken a liking to him."

"But he cannot survive here," Sir Greyson says. "He will die."

"All men die," the black-haired mermaid says. "Some sooner than others."

"But you spared him once," Sir Greyson says.

"For another purpose," the red-haired mermaid says.

"What will you do with him?" Sir Greyson says.

He is beginning to think, dear reader, that he will have to fight the mermaids for the boy. He looks up at the bridge again.

His men stand at the corners, ready to come at his word. Perhaps some of them would be lost. Perhaps he would. Would it be so very bad to die in the arms of a lovely woman, even if she were only half a woman?

He takes another step forward. The mermaids bare their teeth once more.

"He shall be my souvenir," the red-haired one says. "Of another world." She looks around at the woods, the bridge, the grass waving in a wind that, moments ago, did not exist. "A better world."

And then, at that very moment, a golden-haired mermaid breaks the surface of the water. "Arya," she says. "Father has sent for you."

The red-haired beauty sighs. She puts the boy down. "Take him, then," she says, in a voice that sounds as if she has suffered a great defeat. Her eyes are sad. Sir Greyson does not quite understand, but before he can question her further she disappears beneath the surface, along with her sisters.

Sir Greyson waits until they have vanished from sight before he drags his prince's body away from the water. Blood makes the prince's hair sticky. It looks as though it comes from a large wound on the right side of his forehead. Prince Virgil must have fallen and hit his head before slipping into the water. What was the prince doing near this bridge, so close to these mermaids?

"We need a healer," Sir Greyson says to the crowd peering around the bridge.

"There is no healer," a man calls out. A man, Sir Greyson sees, who used to be the village healer. But he has lost his child, and, like the others, will do no favors for the castle until his son is returned.

Sir Greyson picks up his prince's body, limp in his arms, and on his way to the king and queen, he does not meet a single eye of the villagers. He merely bows his head to his king and awaits further instruction.

Traitor

Two months passed, and Greyson's father did not return. But Greyson and his mother carried on. They knew these trips could very well take months, for peace was of highest importance in the realm, at least to the king's men. His father had promised to return before the Year's Last Day, but the day came and went, with little celebration, since many of the village men were soldiers. And with every day passing, the world grew a bit darker for Greyson and his mother.

Greyson could not even find relief in the friendship of Cora, for she continued to pay him no mind. He was fast becoming a man, but she did not watch him as he watched her. They hardly spoke. He left his mother's candies at her door, for he could not bear to see them on his family's table, in the familiar bowl, waiting for his father's return. Sometimes, he would slip a slice of apple pie to Cora's windowsill when the sun had gone to sleep.

One day, she stopped him in the streets. "Why are you leaving me sweets?" she said. "I will grow too large for my dresses."

"Then you can use magic to make them larger," Greyson said, filling, momentarily, with his old, customary merriment.

"A woman cannot simply make her garments larger," Cora said. "It is not becoming."

"You are lovely no matter how large you become," Greyson said.

Cora's eyes turned tender, as if she might cry. He had never seen a look such as this one, from a girl such as she. Might she be falling in love with him? But the moment passed, and they carried on in the same silent way as they had done before.

And then there came the day when Cora kissed him on the cheek. There came the day when her eye turned the vivid color of a springtime field, when she said, "Perhaps there is more to you than I thought," and then she disappeared, her staff tapping the ground in a rhythm that felt right and true to Greyson, who could scarcely move.

That was a day his feet did not even touch the ground, for he was a man in love.

But he would soon forget that feeling of weightlessness, the feeling of warmth, the feeling of hope. For when he returned home, he found his mother on the stone floor.

She had fallen while preparing his dinner, and so smoke gathered in the corners of their cottage. She had burned the soup, for when she fell, she found she could not rise. Greyson lifted his mother and carried her to her bed, opening all the windows in the cottage so the smoke could find escape. He ran as fast as he could to the village apothecary. The apothecary could not move quickly anymore, for he was growing older by the minute, and so it seemed to Greyson that it took hours and hours to reach his mother's bedside again.

The apothecary, Sir Tomas, who had been knighted in his youth for his wonders of medicine, not his wonders of battle, as one might expect, was known as a disagreeable man, having grown ever more disagreeable in his old age. "Perhaps you should make sure she does not fall," he said to Greyson, as if it were the boy's fault that his mother had taken to her bed.

"She has never fallen before," Greyson said. He looked at his mother. Her eyes were closed. Her ankles, crossed on the bed, were swollen. The apothecary uncrossed them, and her eyelids fluttered open.

"Stu?" she said.

Stu was Greyson's father. Greyson felt an ache wrap around his chest, as if someone had hugged him but squeezed far too tightly.

"No, Mother," Greyson said. "I have brought the apothecary to examine you."

"Very well," she said, her voice becoming more breath than voice. "The apothecary." And her eyelids closed again.

The apothecary examined Greyson's mother, poking and prodding, lifting her arms and listening to her heart. Her breath rattled in her chest.

How was it that Greyson had not heard this before? How could it be that he had not noticed she was sick?

"It is the sugar sickness," Sir Tomas said, as if it were something he saw every day. "She will need special medicine."

"But where will I get medicine?" Greyson said. He looked at his mother, at her pale cheeks and the silver hair spread on her pillow. Her eyes opened once more. They were tired and, mostly, sad. Greyson could not bear to look at them.

He knew the answer to his own question, of course. The only place anyone in the kingdom could get medicine was from the palace. It was from the king. Would King Willis give him medicine to cure his mother? His father was the king's captain. Perhaps that would matter.

"Do not ask me, boy," the apothecary said. "I only tell you what is wrong." And then he turned and walked out the door.

As you can see, it is true what I said before: the apothecary was not a very agreeable man. Can you imagine, dear reader, having a healer such as this one?

Greyson held his mother's hand, listening to her labored breathing. "Mother," he finally said. "I must visit the castle."

"Yes," she said, and then she collapsed into a cough so violent it shook the whole bed and Greyson with it. Blood spatters fell from her mouth. "Yes," she said, when she had calmed. A spot of blood remained on her chin.

"Mother," Greyson said, pulling a handkerchief from his pocket and dabbing her chin. "You are bleeding."

She coughed again, this time into the handkerchief. "Yes," she said. She looked at her son, her blue eyes wide and glassy. "I did not want to tell you. We have enough trouble."

"You mean with Father gone?" Greyson said.

"Yes," his mother said.

"But he will return," he said. He kissed the top of his mother's hand. "You should have told me. What if it is too late?"

His mother laughed softly, but it ended in another violent cough. "I fear it may very well be."

"No," Greyson said. He stood. "I shall go now. I will ask the king to help. Father has done his duty. Now the king can do his."

"I am afraid it is not so simple as that," his mother said. "The sugar sickness does not give up so very easily. And neither does our king."

"I will do whatever it takes," Greyson said, for, you see, he loved his mother very much.

"Very well," his mother said. "If you must."

"I will return soon," he said. He bent to kiss his mother, and then he ran as fast as he had ever run in all his life, down the dirt road and over the bridge, past the calling mermaids, and all the way to the door of the castle. He used the bronze knocker, molded into a bear's growling face with a ring held between its teeth, and listened to its echo inside the castle walls. A servant opened the door. Greyson bowed, though he knew this was not the king.

"I need some medicine," he said. "For my mother. My father is the captain of the king's guard, and, as such, his family should have access to whatever they need. It is the king's duty." The words came out in a rush, and he had no way of knowing whether the servant understood him or whether it was all nonsense.

The servant held up a hand. "One moment, please," he said. He shut the door. Greyson waited outside, terrified, trying not to think about every second passing, every second his mother lay on her bed, dying. Then the door opened once more. "Please," the servant said. "Follow me. The king does not wish to see anyone right now, but he has made an exception for you."

Greyson followed the servant to a wide door, which opened onto a large room with ceilings painted in extravagant scenes. A red carpet waited for him, leading the way to the king's throne. King Willis sat on the throne, a large man then, but not overly large as he is today. When Greyson drew close, he saw that the king was eating a sweet roll. King Willis did not offer Greyson refreshment.

"Hello, boy," the king said. "You come here late. I was just about to retire for the eve."

"My mother is sick," Greyson said. "I come on behalf of her." He bowed to the floor. He had never spoken with the king before. He wished he did not need to this moment.

"And your father?" the king said. He did not seem to know that Greyson was the son of the captain.

"He is the captain of your guard," Greyson said. "They are away in Ashvale. You sent them." He tried to keep the accusation out of his voice, but we cannot blame him, can we, dear reader? His beloved father did not make it home for the Year's Last Day, nor did he show up for the Year's First Day, though the king had promised his men they would have, at the very least, these days with their family. Is it so very easy for a king to forget the words he has vowed? Is it so very easy to deny men what they so deserve?

"And what is it about your mother?" King Willis said.

"She collapsed," Greyson said. "She cannot rise from her bed as yet. The apothecary said she has the sugar sickness. He said she needs medicine to live." His words, again, came out in a great rush of emotion, though he tried to control them in front of this man who was his king. The king stared at him, as if uncomprehending. Greyson did not know whether he should say it all again or whether he should remain silent. He had never spoken to a king, remember.

Say something, Your Majesty. Say something to this boy who is worried about his mother and terrified for his father.

The king rose from his throne. He paced before the boy on a plain wooden platform that looked nothing like the king's platform looks today. It was merely an ugly slab of wood. King Willis stopped and held up a finger.

"Let me tell you, boy," the king said. "Let me tell you what has happened. We have not heard a single word from your father since the day his journey began." The king turned his dark eyes upon the boy. "He is a traitor. He has left without a trace."

No. His father would never desert. He would never leave his family. He was an honorable man, a strong man, a man who loved peace and kindness and courage.

"No," Greyson said. "You are wrong."

What words they are to say to a king, would you not agree? To point out a king's error, when you are a boy of seventeen, is not so very wise, one might suppose. But such is the nature of love. Greyson knew his father. He knew he would never do what it was the king said he had done.

"Do not argue with me, boy," King Willis said. His eyes narrowed, and his face grew dark. "He has deserted me." He took a step closer to Greyson, though he was still safe on his platform, feet away from the boy. "He has deserted you."

"No," Greyson said. It was involuntary, creeping out the sides of his mouth. He knew very well that it was quite dangerous to argue with a king. But they were speaking of his father. A boy knew his father, did he not?

Grief stole silently up into Greyson's heart. His father, gone. What would they do? What would they do now? The kingdom was not known to be kind to those who were traitors or those who found themselves connected to traitors. The kingdom was not known to be kind to those who needed kindness most.

"So what is it you desire, boy?" King Willis said.

Greyson sucked in a long breath. Perhaps he could still acquire what it was he needed. "Medicine," he said. He hated the way his voice cracked right down the middle. "For my mother."

"And why should I give you medicine when your father is a traitor?" King Willis turned his shining eyes upon Greyson. They gleamed with disgust or malice or something darker indeed.

"My father is not a traitor!" Greyson said. And he meant it. He meant it like he had meant nothing else in his life.

"Oh, but he is," the king said. His voice grew low and cruel. "He is a traitor of the worst kind, and you will get nothing from me. NOTHING." He gestured to his page, an old man by now, for he had been King Sebastien's unfortunate page. "Get him out of my court."

The page did as he was told. He was still surprisingly strong for an old man. But Greyson patted his hands away, for he did not want to cause any trouble. He would leave easily. So the man took his hands off Greyson as soon as they were out of the king's sight.

The page, who was a kind man in an unfortunate situation, asked the boy to wait at the door. He disappeared for only moments before he returned with a vial. "Here is something that may help with the sugar sickness," he said. "Perhaps this will last until you might figure out what is next."

Greyson nodded, so overcome with emotion he could not speak. But the man seemed to know what he might say, for he smiled and pushed Greyson out the front doors of the castle.

Greyson ran all the way back home, his eyes streaming as he stumbled through the darkness. Not even the moon shone on a night such as this one.

Light

The children stare about them, still trying to find their friend, though she has disappeared without a trace. Only a scrap of cloth remains, a dirty hem from the dress she wore, the portal she restored that has brought them out from their trap beneath the ground.

"We knew," Arthur says. "We knew this could happen." And they are not so much words of comfort as they are words of despair.

"We are saved," Maude says. She wraps an arm around her husband, pulls him close. Hazel weeps behind her. "We will find her. But first we must find safety."

"We cannot leave Mercy!" says the girl called Ursula. Her sea-blue eyes flash. "We must find her.

"No," Maude says. "We must go. She has given herself so that we might be safe."

The ultimate sacrifice, you see. Mercy has disappeared, perhaps given her very life so that twenty-three children and Arthur, like a father to the girl, and Maude, like a kindly aunt, might live. So that they might run.

Arthur pulls in a ragged breath. "Yes," he says. "We must go."

"We cannot," Hazel says. Her eyes, her lips, her hands, her voice, everything about her shakes as if a violent wind blows within. It is the wind of grief. "We cannot leave Mercy." Mercy is her dearest friend. How does one leave one's dearest friend to danger and, possibly, death?

"We must," Arthur says. "We must go. We must run." He looks around, as if expecting the king's men to emerge from the wood's shifting shadows. The woods appear darker now than he remembers. The trees sway, as if their branches are reaching toward the children. "The king's men will return soon." He looks up at the gray sky, peeking in patches through the tops of the trees. "It will grow dark soon."

The children look around, too, behind trees, up into the leaves, behind them, before them, everywhere. There are dangers in these woods that they do not wish to meet with the sun's setting.

"Let us go," Maude says.

"But where?" Hazel says. Her voice is like a tiny mirror,

dropping before them and shattering. "Where can we go?"

The children know as well as Arthur and Maude that the only way to the other kingdoms is back toward Fairendale, and treading back toward Fairendale is much too dangerous now. They would never make it without discovery, not without magic. Where was it, in fact, that Arthur and Maude had thought to hide the children? Was there such a place at all?

Maude and Arthur look at one another. The wind curls through the trees, bending their leaves toward the ground, as if the wood, too, is weeping. In the distance, though they cannot be seen, the king's men are wondering what has happened to the green ball of light. They are turning around. They are searching for the place they have left, for the place the tiny shoe marked.

"We must travel through the lands of Morad," Arthur says. "It is the only way."

The children stare at him. Maude's mouth drops open, and before she can even say a single word, her head gives a small shake. "No," she says. "No. Never. Absolutely not. It is far too dangerous. We would never make it."

The children have never seen the dragon lands. Once upon a time, the dragons and the people of Fairendale were on friendly terms with one another. They were companions, helping one another in the ways that only companions can help one another, which is to say the people provided friendship and love, and the dragons provided backs for travel, and, of course, love in return. But King Sebastien changed all of that the day he marched with two thousand men through the forest, which was not known as the Weeping Woods then but bore only a fraction of the name: The Woods. He stole the castle, slaying far too many dragons to ever hope for reconciliation. To this day, the people and the dragons stay far from each other, following their after-battle agreement to never venture onto one another's land.

So, you see, it could very well be dangerous for the children and Maude and Arthur to travel into the dragon lands. It could very well mean their death, and is it not life they are trying to preserve? Is that not what Mercy intended when she disappeared and did not reappear?

"It is the only way," Arthur says.

"But they will never let us cross," Maude says.

"We do not know for sure," Arthur says.

"We do," Maude says. "It is written in the stories. It is written in our history."

"There are other stories and histories written as well," Arthur says. "About kind hearts and love between humans and dragons."

"Not since the days before King Sebastien," Maude says. "The days of The Good King Brendon."

The children watch Arthur and Maude, turning their heads

from one face to another. They notice that Arthur's eyes have a gleam in them, a gleam that looks similar to hope, perhaps. They notice that Maude's eyes have darkened in what can only be fear. They do not know which to follow. Hope or fear?

"We must try," Arthur says. "No one knows what happens when we cross into dragon territory."

"The dragons will destroy us," Maude says.

"We do not know for sure," Arthur says, and if one knew him well enough, as Maude knows her husband, one might be able to see something else in the gleam of his eyes. Something secret. Something of memory. Something of love. And perhaps this is what moves Maude, what changes her mind just in time, before the king's men have stumbled, again, upon the very clearing where Maude and Arthur and the children stand. She nods her head once.

"Very well," she says. "We shall try."

"Come children," Arthur says, looking at the faces already turned to him. "Let us run."

And they begin their second flight.

Aleen lies awake. Everyone else is sleeping, or so she believes. Until she whispers, "They are going. They are truly going," in typical prophetess fashion, with vague meaning and unknown predictions, though this is not a prediction at all. If you will remember, Aleen has lost her prophet Sight. She cannot see what lies ahead, only what is happening now, out in the realm.

But there is one awake. He finds her hand in the dark, this old, bent, wrinkled man called Yerin.

And somewhere in the dark, a child cries out, "Where are they going?" and another cries out, "Who is going?"

"They are going," Yerin says, "to a place no one has been for a very long time."

"A very long time," Aleen says.

"Who is going?" a child asks again.

"The ones who will save us," Aleen says.

And though the children have no idea what this means, for who often knows what the words of prophets and prophetesses mean, after all, they feel it still.

The dark is a little less dark tonight.

And someone else, someone who will, perhaps, play a large part in their rescue, is coming.

They hear him now, his feet shuffling against the steps.

It is the boy called Calvin. He has, once more, stuffed his

pockets full of provisions, stolen a candle from the cabinet, filled a bowl with water and sealed it as best he can, though even now, he can feel it sloshing out the sides as he steps carefully and, as much as he might, smoothly. He has closed the doors behind him, for he does not want the guards, who were sleeping when he stole past, to know he is here. And so he waits until he has passed fifty-three stairs before he lights the candle he carries. He hopes the children will see the light. He hopes they will take comfort in its glow. He hopes it will last long enough until the next time he can visit.

It has been some days, nearly a week, since he has come last. Cook has not been easy to fool. She is a shrewd woman who noticed the missing provisions he carried down on his last visit. So he has begun eating smaller portions, but asking for larger ones, stuffing them, when Cook's back is turned, in a satchel he keeps forever at his feet. This he carries on his back, and it is stuffed with bread and sweet rolls and raw vegetables (he told Cook he will only eat them raw) of every kind and color. Meat he does not bring, for it does not keep. But vegetables and bread will, perhaps, help the children preserve their strength.

If one could see him now, one might be predisposed to laugh, upon first sight. Calvin, you see, is but a boy, but he has strapped a beard onto the bottom of his chin, held on by a bit of string, covered by his merchant's cap. He is trying, you see, to appear as though he is more than a boy, for boys in the kingdom of Fairendale, at present, are in the greatest danger. Cook has not given him to the king, though you can be sure she has wanted to many times, but she does have a tender heart toward the boy who can cut vegetables in the time it takes her to heat up a pot of water. She needs him, more or less. And she knows that he does not have the gift of magic. What kind of boy would cut vegetables, if he had magic to do it for him?

So Calvin wears his beard, and Cook pretends that he is no longer a boy, but a man, and the kingdom is none the wiser. It is true, perhaps, that he did not need to wear his ludicrous beard down these steps this eve, but he feared he risked questioning by the guards. But the guards fell asleep soon after taking watch, and it was with great ease and silence that Calvin snatched the ring of keys from the belt of one and slipped into the dungeon doors without a single jangle.

One might also see, if one looked at this boy who pretends to be a man, a pillow inside his tunic, folded around his belly. Though it is slightly out of place to see a servant with so bulky a belly, more befitting a king, perhaps, rather than a lowly servant, no one is here to question it. And for that, Calvin is glad.

There are more children in this dungeon beneath the dungeons than this one pillow will satisfy, but perhaps, on another visit, he will bring more, stuffed in other places. There are many pillows scattered throughout the Great Hall. No one will notice them gone, will they?

Calvin is the sort of boy every castle should have. Calvin, you see, takes mercy on everyone he sees. He believes the best about a person. He is the kind of boy who can look at his king and see, not a tyrant, but a decent human being who is making bad decisions. It is not often that one can look at an evil person and believe this about them. It is, in fact, quite difficult to remember that all people, no matter what they do, are simply doing the best they can with what they have. So, too, is our king, Calvin believes. But he also believes that the children in the dungeons beneath the dungeons deserve more than bread and water once a day. So he breaks the king's law, for sometimes breaking a law is permitted—courageous, even—when it is for the greater good.

It is a long way down to the bottom of this dungeon. The children do not see the light until Calvin is very nearly there. And then they glance up. They look around. They can see each other and Aleen and Yerin and all the other prophets who sleep near them. It has been days since the last candle burned out, days spent in darkness that seems all the darker once one has looked upon the light. They are grateful that the boy has returned.

Calvin emerges from the stone walls, as if he is an

apparition. But he is not a boy at all. He is a short, fat man. The children gasp.

Calvin holds out a hand. "It is only I," he says. "Calvin."

"Calvin," Aleen says. Her voice soothes the children. "What is it that has happened to you, Calvin?"

Calvin holds the candle between the bars so that Aleen may take it from his hands. "The king is searching for the missing children," Calvin says. "I must not be a child."

"No," Aleen says. "You must not be a child. And so you have become a short, fat man."

"Yes," Calvin says. "Though I did not intend to become fat." He pulls the pillow from beneath his tunic. "This I brought for all of you." He looks at it, its flattened shape. "I know it is not enough, but perhaps I can bring more."

"Very brave of you, my boy," Aleen says. "Very brave indeed. Thank you."

The children murmur thanks of their own. Calvin holds out his sack of food. "It is not much," he says. "Cook has keen eyes. I take what I can."

Aleen looks at the boy. "And you do not eat," she says.

Calvin drops his eyes to the floor. "I do," he says.

"Not much," she says. She pauses, presses her hand through the steel bar, smoothes the hair from Calvin's eyes. "Tell me, boy, why you do what you do."

Calvin meets her eyes, though he has never been good at this. He looks away, back toward the floor. "Because it is the right thing to do," he says.

"Yes," Aleen says. "And you are merciful." Still she stares at him, as if seeing something there that she did not see before. It is a mystery to everyone but Aleen.

"I would let you all out if I could," he says. He holds up the keys, and it is the first time they jangle in his hands. "But there is no key to fit. I do not know where the king keeps the key to this dungeon."

"It is hidden," Aleen says. "In a place that would be far too dangerous for a boy to go. You must not try."

"Where?" Calvin says, for he is a boy, a boy who is not afraid of anything much. What, after all, would he have to lose? Calvin has never had much to lose in this world.

Aleen shakes her head. "I do not know," she says, though it is clear that she does, in fact, know. Yerin moves to the bars, searches her face. Why would Aleen not tell the boy where the key is hidden? Why does she keep this a secret for herself?

Yerin does not know this hiding place. But he sees, in Aleen's face, that it is quite a dangerous one indeed. And should the boy fail, they would be worse off than before. So he does not urge her to tell.

Calvin hands over the last of the provisions he has smuggled down the steps. "I shall return as soon as I might," he says.

"Thank you, my boy," Aleen says. "Thank you for your courage and your mercy."

Calvin dips his head and turns to go. A child calls out, from the back, "Thank you!" and Calvin does not turn back. He simply smiles to himself, for doing the right thing is, perhaps, the best thing of all.

The darkness closes around him, but he knows the way.

Prince Virgil lies on his back, tucked into his royal bed, the satin covers pulled up to his chin. He has not woken. Queen Clarion sits at his side, murmuring, "Oh, my boy" again and again and again. She is terrified that her boy will not wake, terrified that he is lying here, dying, and she can do nothing at all in the world to help him.

The stories say that mermaids have healing powers, that a single touch from them can bring a man back from the brink of death, if that touch is made above water, that is. And she saw with her own eyes that her son was held in the arms of not one, but three mermaids. They spared him. They healed him. This she believes. Every few moments she puts her cheek to her son's chest, feeling the pulse of him vibrate through her head, just to make sure it is still there. She is the only one in his room, the only one who will, now, watch his eyes flutter, witness him wake, see him try to sit up and lie, nearly as quickly, back down.

"Oh, my boy!" Queen Clarion says again. And this time they are not words of terror, they are words of great and unspeakable relief. Joy that runs down her cheeks. Love that swells into her fingertips. She does not hug him, however, though she wants nothing more at this moment, but she knows that moving him might very well aggravate the wound on his head, the wound that has been patched by none other than herself, for the village healer refused to do the work himself. And she could not blame him. He has lost a son. Why would he save another?

Queen Clarion strokes her boy's hair. He winces. His eyes blink at her, as if he cannot see her at all, but something else entirely.

"Where am I?" he says.

"In your bedchambers, dear," she says. She tries not to feel worry at his confusion. Head wounds are confusing things, sometimes disorienting a person until the world settles clear. Perhaps he merely needs time to let it settle.

He looks around his room, and she sees the recognition slip into his eyes. There. It is all very well.

"What happened?" Prince Virgil says.

"That we would surely like to know," Queen Clarion says, and her voice, at the very end of it, cracks. Her joy, you see, holds tears, but she tries her best to keep them away from her son. It is overwhelming, dear reader, to see a living, breathing, speaking person where moments before was a son trapped by a head wound. It is overwhelming to know that life still remains in the one you have feared lost. "Do you remember anything, dear?"

Prince Virgil stares at his mother. His eyes glaze again. "I went out," he says.

"Yes," she says. "This morning?"

He shakes his head, and the pain pulls across his face. "No," he says. "Last eve."

"Last eve?" Queen Clarion says. She had come to wish him goodnight and fair dreams last eve, as she did every eve. He had curled up in his bed and slept. "I thought it was surely this morning." Had her son truly been beneath the bridge all night? Had he passed so many hours with his head weeping?

"I meant to go into the forest," he says.

Queen Clarion draws in a sharp breath. "Whatever for?" she says.

"To find Theo," Prince Virgil says. "And Hazel and Mercy."

Queen Clarion thinks on this for a moment. She thinks

about the question that immediately skips through her mind, the question that frightens her, the question that cannot be answered, here, now, today, the question that could mean hope or despair.

Did he intend to find his friends so he could turn them over to his father, or did he intend to find them so he could save them?

It turns out, however, that she need not ask, for Prince Virgil volunteers this information. "I wished to keep them safe," he says. "I wished to help them escape."

Oh, dear reader. One cannot describe the surprise and wonder, and, yes, hope, again, that wake in Queen Clarion's heart. She wonders if this boy might be braver than his father. If he might be kinder. If he might be a more loving ruler than Fairendale has seen since the days of The Good King Brendon. Might it be so? Could a good boy be born of an evil man?

"My boy," she says, for there is nothing more to say.

"I did not make it," he says.

"You fell before you reached the forest," she says.

"No," he says. "I made it to the forest. I could not make myself enter." He looks at her, and his eyes are so full of pain that she takes his hand and brings it to her lips. "Is there any news of them?"

Queen Clarion shakes her head. "The kingdom was

concerned with finding you," she says. "I noticed you missing this morning." She does not add the part about fearing him dead, for this is not a thing a mother should tell her child.

"And what happened at the forest?" she says.

"Noises," Prince Virgil says. "Creatures. I turned and ran. I must have stumbled."

"On the bridge," she says.

"How am I here?" he says.

"Mermaids," she says. "You were saved by mermaids."

He looks at her questioningly, for he knows the stories better than most. He has grown up in a castle where right outside its doors is a cove of mermaids. He was warned at a very young age to avoid them.

"How is that so?" Prince Virgil says.

Queen Clarion shakes her head. "I do not know, dear," she says. "You were found in the arms of mermaids."

They are quiet for a long time. And then Queen Clarion says, "My brave boy."

"I did not do anything," Prince Virgil says, and his voice holds the smallest touch of anger. "I did not save my friends."

"But you tried," Queen Clarion says. "It is enough to try." She does not want her boy to try again, you see. And her words are, in fact, truer than one might suppose. It is enough to try.

"And they have not been found?" Prince Virgil says.

"Not as yet," Queen Clarion says. She pats her boy's hand. "And we shall hope that they continue eluding the captain and his men."

"The captain does not wish to find them, either," says Prince Virgil. "I have seen it in his eyes."

Queen Clarion nods. Her beautiful face grows sad. "Yes," she says. "He is a good man."

Prince Virgil says nothing.

"Now you must rest," Queen Clarion says. "I will join your father in court today."

"To hear news?" Prince Virgil says.

Queen Clarion nods. "To hear news," she says.

"And you will tell me?" Prince Virgil says.

"Yes," she says. "Once you rest."

Queen Clarion does not leave her son's bedchambers even after he closes his eyes and slips into sleep.

So it is that Queen Clarion misses the entrance of the captain in late afternoon. She is still with her boy, still easing him into sleep, when Sir Greyson makes his presence known to his king, who is sleeping on his throne, his chin tucked all the way into the folds of his neck, by clearing his throat. Our good man does not want to deliver the news he has been given, for he is well aware of the king's wrath, particularly when it comes to losing the missing children once they have been found.

But he does his duty.

"What do you mean they have been lost once more?" The king's voice echoes in the empty room, bouncing off the walls and blowing back into the captain's face. Garth, along a side wall, shivers, but Sir Greyson does not move. He is a man of valor, after all. He stands as still as he might in front of his king, as if he is a statue made of metal.

"There is nothing we can do," Sir Greyson says again. "We have returned to the place where the shoe was found, but there is only flattened grass, where it seems many feet stood before fleeing."

"They have escaped you again!" The king roars. "How is it possible that they have escaped you again?"

"Half my men were looking for your son," Sir Greyson says. And half of them were chasing a glowing green orb, this he does not say aloud. It sounds foolish even to him, though he must admit that when Sir Merrick told him about the floating ball, he, too, thought it was very surely magic. For balls do not float of their own accord. But a ball that pops in flight? He could not understand what his men meant when they told the story of its disappearing. They had, however, left the place where the children hid unattended, and this is why they lost, once again, the ones for whom they have been looking.

Though Sir Greyson does not believe the losing is a bad turn of events at all. If it were not for his men and how exhausted they are, he would be very glad indeed. The longer the children are safe from the hands of the king, the better. He would never tell his king that, of course.

"We did not need half your men here at the castle," the king shouts in his captain's face.

"We did not know, sire," Sir Greyson says. "Someone made the call. We believed it was dire."

King Willis paces the stage. He did not know what had happened to his son, but perhaps he did not need to use the dire signal. Perhaps he could have ordered the less dire call. Perhaps it would have left more men in the forest and the children would not have slipped away.

"Perhaps you should have commanded your men to stay put," King Willis says, for he is not a man who much likes blame, particularly when it falls upon himself.

This is the part Sir Greyson has been dreading, but he must tell the king now or risk his men looking incompetent, which, despite what some may think, is not true in the least.

"My men," Sir Greyson says, "discovered a ball of magic. They thought the children might be hiding inside, so they chased it."

"A ruse!" King Willis shouts. "Any man would know it was a trick."

In truth, dear reader, one could not know. There were stories of magicians who had used the very same trick to carry a multitude of people across a great distance so they might invade another land. Some sorcerers, in fact, had used a glowing ball to cross the Violet Sea, for no creature could penetrate a sorcerer's orb.

Sir Greyson, good man he is, drops his head. "Yes, sire," he says. "I suppose any man would."

"And now you have lost the children once more!" King Willis says. "It is unacceptable."

Sir Greyson does not say anything. He believes it is coming now, his dismissal. He will not be able to help his mother after all. But perhaps he will be able to save the children. This thought brings him great hope.

"Where are your men now?" King Willis says.

"In the woods, sire," Sir Greyson says. "Watching the place where the children were hiding."

"If they have already escaped, what is the point of watching?" King Willis says.

Sir Greyson does not say that there is, in fact, nothing else to do. The grass had been flattened where the children emerged from wherever it was they were hiding, but there are no tracks leading anywhere. His men have searched long and hard. It is as if the children have disappeared into the air.

King Willis walks across the platform. Sir Greyson has never seen the king move so much. It is quite a sight to see, to be honest—that bright, shining purple robe trailing behind the king's every step, catching the light, distorting it in places as though the robe is more prism than solid material. Sir Greyson is mesmerized by the king's movements. He cannot raise his eyes to his king's face, because of that robe. Not that King Willis notices. Remember, dear reader? He does not notice much about other people. He does not notice, either, what a spectacle he is, with his round body and his fancy clothes and his plate of sweet rolls, waiting within reach. He does not know that the people in his kingdom, the people in this very castle, turn away from this greedy man and shake their heads for the simple fact that he has so much and all the others have so little.

He does not know.

And would he care?

What a sad answer that is.

No, dear reader. He would not care at all. For our king, the Great and Mighty King Willis, believes he is a good and strong and noble king. And perhaps he could be, had he lived another life. Perhaps he could be, had he been able to break free from his father's hold.

Whatever does his father have to do with him now? you might ask. His father is dead.

Well, the dead do not always remain dead, you see. But that is a story for later. For now, Sir Greyson must answer his king.

"We do not know for certain that they have escaped," Sir Greyson says.

"Well," the king says. "Well." He turns this way and that, slow and heavy. "We must find them." He looks at his captain. "We must find them immediately."

"Yes, sire," Sir Greyson says. "My men are trying."

"Have you searched the entire forest?" King Willis says.

"My men are doing that as we speak," Sir Greyson says. As soon as Prince Virgil was found, Sir Greyson sent his men back to their task, though he fears it is too late.

And, yet, he does not fear it at all, but merely rejoices, for children escaping means children could very well be safe once more.

"Go," King Willis says. "Go join them. Do not come back to me without news." King Willis turns to face Sir Greyson once more, sweeping his eyes over the captain's armor. "Make it good news."

Sir Greyson bows. "Yes, sire," he says, and he is just about to leave his king's presence when King Willis stops him with a word.

"Captain," King Willis says.

"Yes, sire," Sir Greyson says.

"Those mermaids," King Willis strokes his chin. It is smooth, as it has always been. King Willis does not grow a beard as many in his kingdom do. He thinks it is unbecoming.

Sir Greyson's eyes lock with the king's. "The ones by the bridge, Your Majesty?" Sir Greyson says.

"How long have they been here?" King Willis says, ignoring Sir Greyson's question.

"I do not know, sire," Sir Greyson says. "I believe they come visit us every year. Their father is said to be king of the Violet Sea."

"King of the Violet Sea," King Willis says. "Imagine that."

Yes. Imagine that. King of all the horrors the great sea hides in its depths. Were there dangers for that kind of king, or did he live in relative comfort?

"Why do they come?" King Willis says.

"It is believed that they seek men," Sir Greyson says, though he is merely repeating the stories his mother told him as a boy. No one, you see, knows much about mermaids at all, but for what is known from the stories.

"And why do they seek men, pray tell?" King Willis says.

"For their kingdom, perhaps?" Sir Greyson says.

It is one of the great mysteries of the land. Stories tell of men who, so entranced by the beauty of the mermaids, walked willingly into their waters and their arms, never to be seen again. But no one knows, alas, what happens once a man's head disappears beneath the sea.

"What do you think they wanted with my son?" King Willis says, and for the first time, Sir Greyson can see a bit of the king's humanity, for his voice has raised a pitch, as if fear rides on his words.

"Prince Virgil touched their waters," Sir Greyson says. "They believed him to be theirs."

"And how was it that you convinced them otherwise?" King Willis says. His black eyes watch his captain closely.

Sir Greyson measures his words. He does not, of course, know why the mermaids gave Prince Virgil to him so willingly, but does he want his king to know this?

"They were called away, sire," he says, for it is the only explanation he can recall.

"They were called away," King Willis says. He does not say anything for a while. Sir Greyson is not certain that he may go, so he remains as is. And King Willis does have something else to say, for he looks once more at his captain and says, "They should not be in my domain."

It is so unexpected that Sir Greyson cannot help but say,

"But the waters were given them long ago."

"They are my waters," King Willis says, his hand waving in the air. "Just as Fairendale is my land."

Sir Greyson does not, in fact, know what to say. The mermaids have been in the tributary for thousands of years, so the stories say. "But sire—" he tries once more.

"They are not welcome here," King Willis says.

"But—" King Willis only allows his captain one word before he finishes.

"They tried to take my son," King Willis says.

"They let him go," Sir Greyson says.

"He may not be so fortunate next time," King Willis says. "It is your duty to protect the kingdom. There is no kingdom without my son." The king's voice echoes into the silence that follows. Sir Greyson cannot, in truth, find a single word to say. He merely stares at his king, his mouth dropping open a bit, which would not have mattered quite so much if he had remembered to return his knight's helmet to his head. But now the king can see his shock, and perhaps this is what makes him say the worst of all words.

"You will drive them from the waters."

Sir Greyson involuntarily shakes his head.

"Yes," the king says. "You shall do as I say. Or you will be relieved of your duties."

If one were to see inside the head of this captain, standing before his king, one might see something like this:

It is not possible.

What you are asking would be far too dangerous.

It would demand my very life.

I cannot give my life. There is my mother.

There is my mother. How will she live if I do not do this?

There is my mother.

There is my mother.

There is my mother.

Poor Sir Greyson. He is caught, you see, for he cares more for his mother than he cares for his very life. For her, he would do anything.

And so it is that Sir Greyson finds his head nodding, instead of shaking. And with the nodding, all thoughts vanish from his head, but for one: "Which shall I do first," he says. "Shall I find the children or drive the mermaids from their waters?"

"From *my* waters," King Willis growls. And then he laughs. He laughs until there is no sound left in the royal throne room. "You ask what you should do first," the king says when he has quite finished laughing. "You ask the king what it is you should do first, as if one is not clearly more important than the other." His eyes are narrow and hard, his voice like a cold wind shaking the room in its gust. "Find the children."

And he waves his arm, as if casting Sir Greyson from his presence.

Sir Greyson turns and strides away, his face warm and cold all at the same time.

The king's roaring laughter follows him out the front doors of the castle.

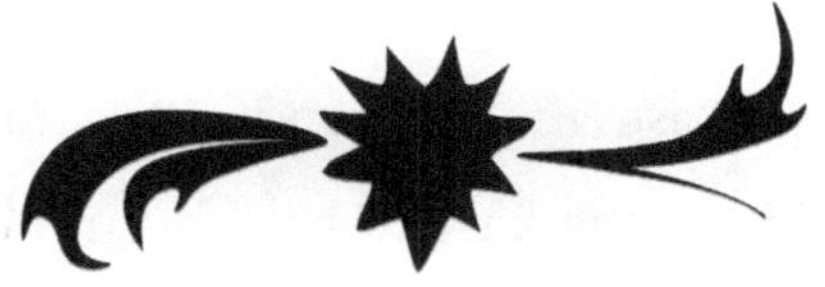

Captain

It was not so very long before his father's men showed up at Greyson's door, the same day he happened to run out of medicine for his mother. "You have returned," he said, looking around for his father. He did not find it odd that his father's men were the ones who had come to his door, not his father. Grief, you see, can make a man blind as well as foolish for a time. Greyson had been so consumed with caring for his mother that he had not given another thought to what the king had said of his father, though his nights were filled with nightmares.

The front man, a large bulky man his father called Miller, dropped to a knee. "We are sorry," he said, and that was all, but it was enough. Oh, yes. It was enough.

Greyson stood before him, his throat growing dry. "What is it?" he said, though he very well knew, for a son always knows.

"Your father," said another man, the one his father had

always called Green. "He did not come back with us."

"So he did desert the king?" Greyson whispered.

The men stared him, their faces twisted in confusion. And then Miller said, "No. Your father would never desert." And Greyson felt hope rise in him again. His father was not a deserter. He could ask the king to help his mother. He could go back. It was within his rights, as long as his father worked for the king.

But his hope did not last so very long, for Green said, "There was a volcano. Ashvale is a land of fire mountains, you will recall."

"But fire mountains are not dangerous," Greyson said, for there had never been danger before. "They are merely mountains with holes cut all the way through them."

The men looked at one another. "This one was dangerous," Green said. "This one spit fire from its bowels."

They told the story in pieces.

"We tried to get everyone safely out," one man said.

"But your father returned for those who could not walk," another man said.

"He was a brave man," still another said.

"He saved many, many people," Green said. "But he did not make it out himself."

They stood there while Greyson wept, trying to understand

what they were telling him, trying to figure out what this might mean for him and his mother, trying to reconcile the long, searing ache that began in his chest and spread all the way to his toes and the tips of his fingers. He took a step back from the doorway. All the men fell to their knees. They bowed.

"We are yours to command," they said with one voice.

Miller raised his eyes to look at Greyson. "You are very like your father," he said. "Good and kind and brave. We would be honored if you would lead us."

"But I am not even yet a man," Greyson said. "I am only seventeen."

"It matters not," Miller said. "We knew your father. We know you will follow in his footsteps."

"But I do not want to lead an army," Greyson said. He had his mother to care for, after all. How would he keep her alive if he were gone from her bedside?

How would he keep her alive if he did not do what it was the men were asking? He would have no medicine, and she would surely die without that.

"Your mother is very sick," Green said. "We heard the talk on the way in to town. She will die without medicine. And the only way you can get medicine…" He let his voice trail off, for he knew the boy already knew.

"Is to work for the king," Greyson said. He could scarcely

breathe, though the door was open and the air was crisp and fresh. Yes. He would have to work for the king. He had no other choice. He could not let his mother die.

The men stood. "We are on our way to the king," Green said. He held out his hand for Greyson to shake. Greyson hesitated before taking it. "We will inform him of your plans." Greyson could only nod, his entire body lost to numbness. He did not feel Green's hand. He did not feel his feet on the ground of his family's cottage. He did not feel the heart thumping in his chest.

The men left, and Greyson moved to close his door. He did not see Cora until she spoke. "So a captain," she said.

His throat felt tight, for this was something he never wanted to be. But love will do curious things to a man's ideals. "Yes," he said.

"You will work for that horrible man," Cora said. She looked at him with those sharp eyes that could cut all the way through him.

"I must," he said. She must understand. There was nothing more he could do for his mother but lead these men in their army.

"There are other ways," Cora said. She tilted her head, as if challenging him.

"No," Greyson said. "There are none."

"If you could see," Cora said.

Greyson shook his head. "I do not see another way," he said. "Tell me, please, if there is another way."

Cora moved to him in a whisper. She put her hand on his arm. "Magic," she said. Her eyes flashed. He felt their jolt in the pit of his stomach.

"There is no magic to fix sickness," he said.

Her eyes flickered again. "But there is," she said. "When you find someone whose magic is strong enough."

"But no one has ever lived with strong enough magic to cure sickness," Greyson said.

Cora did not answer. She merely took a step back.

"There is no time to waste on silly stories," Greyson said. "This is the only way. It is the only way to save my mother."

"I see," Cora said. She took another step back, dissolving into shadow.

"I will still see you," Greyson said.

"What does it matter, boy?" Cora said. Her voice was angry, cruel once more. "You are nothing to me."

He could not see her any longer. He stepped outside the door of his cottage.

"Cora," he said.

"Do not speak to me," she said. "You are nothing to me."

He moved ever forward, but she was gone, disappeared into

the darkness so quickly he did not even see her retreat. Overhead, a blackbird screeched, letting loose the saddest cry the world had ever heard.

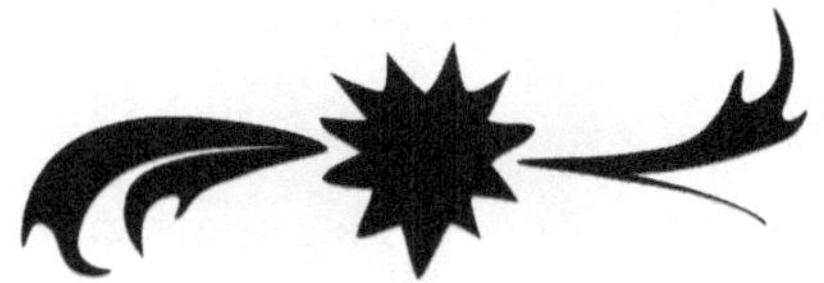

Morad

Prince Virgil wakes with a start. It is a nightmare that pulls him from his deep and peaceful sleep. He wakes crying out, and it startles his mother, who dozes in the chair just beside his bed.

"What is it, Virgil?" Queen Clarion says.

"Mermaids," he says. "There were mermaids in my nightmares. Not like the ones in the cove."

Queen Clarion strokes his cheek. "What about the mermaids?" she says, for she knows that the mermaids in his dream were very much like the mermaids in the cove. The mermaids in the cove have not yet shown their true selves to her boy.

"They were reaching for me," Prince Virgil says. "Fighting over me. There was one with red hair."

Oh, yes. Queen Clarion had seen the mermaid with red hair, the one who held Prince Virgil in her arms and would not let go.

"And there were others?" Queen Clarion says.

"Three others," Prince Virgil says. "With black hair and sharp teeth." He shivers beneath his covers. Queen Clarion touches his hair.

"You are safe," she says. "The mermaids cannot get you here."

"Why did they let me go?" Prince Virgil says, and before his mother can answer, he moves on. "What if I should fall again?"

Queen Clarion is silent for a time. Truth be told, she does not know why her son was let go, but she is grateful. She looks at her son, but he is lost in the nightmare. She takes his hand. "Virgil," she says, and his eyes raise to hers, so like his fathers and yet so very different. Gentler, perhaps. She cannot say for sure. "You have lived in this castle for twelve years. You have never fallen before."

She does not say that he has never before ventured out at night, but Prince Virgil understands. The night is dangerous. Perhaps it was not always so. But he knows it today.

His mother's eyes flicker in the candlelight. "You are safe now," she says.

Prince Virgil looks away, toward the talisman he has buried in a chest. Perhaps he should take to wearing it again. Perhaps it would provide an extra layer of safety. Perhaps it might one day save him.

If only our prince could know. If only.

"There was one," Prince Virgil says, as if thinking aloud. "The red-haired one. She sang over me."

"In your dream?" Queen Clarion says.

Prince Virgil shakes his head and winces. His head is not yet healed, for wounds like these take time. "No. I remember."

"What did she sing over you?" Queen Clarion says.

"It was not a song of our land," Prince Virgil says. He peers at his mother, searching for the smallest clue. Her face does not change. "Perhaps it was a song from her land."

Still he searches. And he is rewarded, for there it is, just a short darkening of her eyes, and then they return to their clear blue. What is it about the mermaid's song that could bring fear to a mother's heart?

"Let us not speak of mermaids," Queen Clarion says, for perhaps she knows what her son has discovered in her eyes.

"She had a lovely voice," Prince Virgil says. "It was warm. And safe."

Queen Clarion leans forward, as if to make sure her son does not miss her words. "It was not safe," she says. Her voice is soft, yet hard. "A mermaid's voice is never safe."

"She had the largest blue eyes I have ever seen," Prince Virgil says. "While the others were fighting, she held on. She would not let them have me."

"It was a trick," Queen Clarion says. "Nothing more."

Prince Virgil does not argue, for how does one argue with a mother and stories? Mermaids were never safe in any of the tales. How could it be that a safe one had found him?

"Tell me a story, Mother," Prince Virgil says. Perhaps she will tell him something of value in a story.

"What kind of story, Virgil?" Queen Clarion says. It is clear that she is pleased with his asking, for Prince Virgil is growing up, and he does not often ask to hear his mother's stories any longer. She has so many to tell, you see. So many that could keep him safe from other dangers besides mermaids. Dangers such as losing one's bearings in the grip of power. Dangers such as believing one is better than another simply for one's station in life. Dangers such as listening to the counsel of one's father when one's father is King Willis or worse.

"A story of mermaids," Prince Virgil says.

Queen Clarion tilts her head, and her eyes narrow of their own accord. "I thought we might be done with mermaids," she says.

"I want to hear a true story," he says. "Do you know one?"

Yes. Queen Clarion does know one. But she does not know if her son is ready to hear this one yet.

"Perhaps I should tell you another story," Queen Clarion

says. "One about your uncle."

"I want to hear a story of mermaids," Prince Virgil says, and it is quite clear to Queen Clarion that he will not rest until she has satisfied his curiosity. And so, perhaps, it is precisely the right time for this story.

"Once I knew a man who was taken by the mermaids," Queen Clarion says.

Prince Virgil's eyes narrow. "Is this a true story?" he says.

"Yes," Queen Clarion says. "Did I not say it was?"

"But you came here when you were just a little girl," Prince Virgil says.

"Yes. I did," Queen Clarion says.

"How was it you came to know a man besides my father and my grandfather?" he says.

She does not remind him that she also knew his uncle, for his father has been telling him stories as well, not the kind Queen Clarion tells, but the darker sort, the ones that hold Prince Wendell up as a villain and nothing more.

"It was quite a long time ago," Queen Clarion says. "I was very young."

They are quiet for some minutes before Queen Clarion says, "Shall I go on?" Prince Virgil nods, and she shifts in her chair.

"This man was sailing across the Violet Sea, on his way to another land to see about some velvet for a gown or two for his daughter. He was often gone from home on journeys such as this, and his daughter missed him so. Her mother, you see, worked long hours at the the village bakery, and so much of the time, she was left alone. She grew lonely without her father at home. This time she begged him to let her go with him, but the seas, he said, were far too dangerous. He could not let his beloved daughter even touch them." Queen Clarion pauses for a time, trying not to let the story take hold of her. She had not told this one for some time.

"He was right," she says. "The seas *were* dangerous, for one day he did not come back."

"What happened to him?" Prince Virgil says.

Though it was years ago, Queen Clarion still remembers the day as if just yesterday she were five years old. She had been sweeping their cottage when the captain of the ship her father had sailed away on knocked on her door, back early from what should have been a two-month journey. She had looked around for her father, but the man's voice had stopped her cold.

"He was a very brave man," Queen Clarion says, a long crack climbing down her voice. "He tried to save one of the ship's men from the hands of a mermaid." She remembered thinking that if she had only been there, if he had only been slightly less honorable, perhaps he might have lived.

"What was it about the mermaid?" Prince Virgil says. "Her

beauty?"

Queen Clarion looks at her son. Perhaps it is time to tell him. Perhaps it might save him where she could not save her father. "It is their song," she says. "It is their song that drags a man to the depths of the ocean."

Prince Virgil's eyes widen at the thought. Perhaps he is thinking of that safe, warm song that is not so very safe or warm at all. Perhaps he is measuring what might have been.

"Who was this man?" Prince Virgil says.

Queen Clarion hesitates. She has never told her son the story of his grandfather. She hesitates to do so now. "A man who lived in the town where I grew up," she says.

"And he never came back," Prince Virgil says.

"No," she says. "He never came back."

"But you do not know if he lives or if he died?" Prince Virgil says.

"Had he lived, he would have come back," Queen Clarion says, forgetting herself for a moment.

"How do you know?" Prince Virgil says. "Perhaps his life under water was better than the one above."

The words tremble in Queen Clarion, for it is something she has considered from time to time, but something no daughter ever wants to admit is true. "He did not go willingly," she says, and this is where she always ends. "He tried to save one of the sailors and was pulled under himself."

They do not speak again for some minutes. The candles flicker across the walls, drawing long shadows into their light.

"Now," Queen Clarion says. "Would you like to hear a happier story?" For she has many of those.

Prince Virgil lies back on his pillow. He scratches at the bandage on his head. "No," he says. "I believe I would like to sleep."

"As you wish," Queen Clarion says. "Would you like me to stay as I did before?" Her voice is tender and kind.

"No," Prince Virgil says. "I am much better."

"But the nightmares," Queen Clarion says. She kneels now at the side of her son's bed. His hand is warm in hers.

"I will use my bell if another comes," Prince Virgil says.

He does not say, but he would like nothing more than to be left alone, for it is the talisman he desires to retrieve, but he does not want his mother to see. Not for the secret it might keep between them but simply because he does not want to answer her question. Truth be told, his head has begun throbbing, and that makes it difficult to think.

"Very well, then," Queen Clarion says. She kisses her son on his cheek and stands, her skirt swishing her out the door. "Sleep well."

Prince Virgil waits until his mother shuts his door and he is sure she has moved back down the hall to her own chambers. And only then does he steal out of bed, his vision blurry still, and rummage through the chest of fine clothes and blankets until his hand closes on the blackbird talisman. He ties it round his neck and tucks it beneath the collar of his shirt.

And though it is quite some time before Prince Virgil finds sleep, it is a good, long, deep sleep without a single nightmare.

Arthur and Maude and the children run through the forest as fast as they can, knowing that Mercy saved them from some danger they cannot yet see. They must outrun it before it returns. Tom and Lina ride in the pocket of Arthur's shirt, but the other children do as well as they can, dodging trees and stumbling over stones and trying to remain as quiet as the forest around them.

Why is the forest quiet? This is the question that moves Arthur's feet faster than they have moved in nearly all of his life.

It might surprise you that the children do not mind this running as much as they might under different circumstances. Though there is danger, of course, the children have spent so many days trapped beneath the ground, with nowhere to play or stretch or run, if they so desired, that this is precisely what they have been wanting for quite some time. They are, indeed, so very glad to feel the ache in their legs and the burn in their chest. They are so very glad they can scarcely stop themselves from smiling and giggling and playing. The wind tears across their cheeks. They will all be red-faced by the time this is all over, and they will have to find water, for everyone knows that running at the pace Arthur and Maude and the children run at this moment, right now, requires water. But no one is thinking of this just now. They are merely thinking of running.

Oh, they have missed this so.

Never mind that they are running for their lives.

They run and run and run, past all the weeping trees, past the dangers the forest is said to hold, though it has grown silent in their stead, past the strange-looking flowers and the colorful grasses. They do not see the fairies, said to steal children if they dare venture into the forest, though Arthur keeps a diligent watch for them, prepared to swat them away should they appear. It looks as though no child will be taken to the Lost World today.

They do not see the giant cats that are said to live in the trees, with spots and eyes that glow in the shadows and a smile that curves up like a fingernail moon. They do not see the goblins or the birds or the dryads or any of the forest's creatures. They see only trees with bark and without faces and what is there before them: green grass, a spattering of flowers, and, now, an opening.

As suddenly as their running begins, it ends. Arthur, in the lead, has only to hold up his hand. They all skid to a stop. There is only silence now.

"The boundary line," he says.

The children do not know this boundary line. They have never been this far, you see. They have never, in fact, been inside the forest, for the stories kept them out. So they wait to step across, for the look on Arthur's face says they must.

There is a strange sensation in all of them, a shiver, a pulling back and away from this boundary line, as if something in the forest is not yet ready for them to leave it. Something pulls them back into the woods, back toward Fairendale, back toward danger.

"Wait," Arthur says.

Hazel gazes across the barren land before them. The children have never seen a land so stark and empty and brown. Where are the trees? Where is the beauty? Where is the color? This land is filled with dust and rocks that are larger than they are and mountains in the distance the same color as the land, as if Morad could not think of a single color to brighten its landscape. This does not look like a land with water or food or anything that might guarantee life. It looks like a wasteland, in fact.

"What is this land?" Hazel says.

Arthur takes a breath. "Morad," he says. "We have reached the land of Morad." His voice is soft, as if he is gazing out on something spectacular rather than a colorless desert. "The land of dragons."

Were Arthur and Maude and the children to look around, perhaps they might see a man, watching. Perhaps they might see his face only, for his body is dressed in bark and leaves and anything that might make him more invisible, more effectively hidden, more conspicuous. He has perfected this disguise, over many days, and now it looks as he always thought it would look —as if he is a walking tree.

He is disguised, you see, as a dryad.

Dryads, in the stories of old, are spirits that live in the trees, spirits with faces and, sometimes, hands. This man has become one, though not really. His becoming is quite contrived.

The unknown man watches Arthur and Maude and the children. His breath comes in puffs, silent, but streaming a momentary fog before him. He has only just stopped running as well, but his footfalls were silent. The children's were quite thunderous, you see, so they had no idea that he followed them.

Not even Arthur, who prides himself on hearing what others cannot (though you will remember that he did not hear the king's men coming for the children that fateful eve not so very long ago. He would say it was the wind and the rain that masked those hooves, but one can never be sure.).

Maude, who has a better nose than any animal of these woods, does not even smell this stranger, for he has packed dirt and earth and leaves so efficiently that he does not hold a scent of humanity.

And so he stands, undiscovered.

He watches. He waits.

He hunts.

There is another who hunts as well.

Of course all those waiting at the border of the dragon lands cannot see him, but Death is here. Death waits. His black robes, by their very nature, keep him hidden. He does not speak. He does not move. He merely waits behind the trees with a grin that would frighten even the bravest of men, for it is a grin that belongs to a skeleton, with a hole for a mouth and little else, except for those white teeth gleaming from the shadows like garish lights. Perhaps it is better that he is invisible.

Death waits for what is to come.

Rounds

So it was that Greyson, that good, brave, kind boy, became Sir Greyson. He stood before King Willis and pledged his honor and life and duty to the king's wishes and the kingdom's safety, and he led his men into peaceful lands and protected the kingdom from the invisible dangers that the king liked to fabricate so that he could assure the people of Fairendale that he was caring for their best interests, always.

Cora married a merchant man, a sailor who treated her kindly, and they bore a daughter together, a beautiful daughter with flaming hair and grassy eyes, every bit as talented as her mother before her.

And every now and again, when Sir Greyson made the rounds of the town at night, for there was not much for his men to do in those days, he would watch Cora through her window, sleeping soundly, alone. And he would wonder.

It is wonder, dear reader, that kept him alive, until the time of our present story.

Step

The children are still wondering about this boundary line. They are still wondering what it might possibly hold for them. Life? Or certain death?

"Why here?" Hazel says. "Why must we go here?"

"It is the only way across," Arthur says. "Into the land of Rosehaven."

The only way across.

Desperation will make a man do things he might never do without it.

It is more than a little frightening to consider the problem with this plan. Arthur and Maude and the children stand at the very boundary of lands that have not been crossed since King Sebastien stole the throne from The Good King Brendon and drove all the dragons from their place beside humans. King Sebastien could not trust the dragons, you see, for they fought on the side of The Good King Brendon. And from that day forward, the dragons were forbidden to step into the land of Fairendale, just as the people of Fairendale were forbidden to step into the lands of Morad.

The dragons and humans lived in harmony once upon a time. But, alas, that is a long time past.

So it is with trepidation that any foot might cross this boundary, for no one knows whether the dragons live or whether they disappeared when they could no longer find purpose in the lives of humans. But if they have not disappeared, well then, Arthur, Maude and all these children are defying an agreement made long ago.

Arthur stares at the line, the green giving way to brown sand. He grabs the hand of his wife, who grabs her daughter's, who grabs Chester's and on and on and on down the line.

Once they move, there is no turning back. Arthur knows this. They could all die in these lands, and no one would know. The dragons, right now, could be waiting. They could be hiding behind the peaks of mountains or in the oversized caves, waiting to destroy them with great puffs of fire, and how might he, Arthur, feel, watching all the children, who have come so very far, who have lived in spite of all the odds against them, disappear in a cloud of smoke?

And yet it is true. They have come so far. They have escaped the king's men. They cannot turn back now. To turn back now would be to certainly die, and while it is probably certainly death to continue forward, they cannot risk anything but this.

Fate, it seems, has been on their side. Perhaps it will be still.

Arthur stares. He thinks. He takes a deep breath. He looks at his wife.

"Ready?" he says.

Maude's eyes are large, but she nods. "Ready," she says.

The children around them shift.

"We all understand that we could die," Arthur says.

The children nod.

"I do not know what will happen once we cross the line," Arthur says.

The children nod again.

He looks from one of them to another, staring at their faces, meeting their eyes. They must make it. They must.

"I love you all," Arthur says. "I truly do. Every single one of you."

They nod again, waiting for him to tell them it is time.

He closes his eyes, so, of course, they all do, too.

And then, as if they are one single body, one person held together by muscle and bone and sinew, they step across the boundary line.

Don't miss out on the next Fairendale adventure!

Will the dragons allow the children to cross Morad? Find out in Book 4: *The Dragons of Morad*.

How to Survive an Encounter with Mermaids

By Jared
A Wanderer on the Violet Sea

I suppose you have heard of the dangers that exist on the surface and down below the Violet Sea. Every child is told all manner of tales about this deathly body of water.

You may also have heard that no one has been able to survive a sailing trip across the Violet Sea. I tell you that is only folklore, however. Not the part about the dangers, but the part about the sailing. I tell you this because I and many others have been sailing on the Violet Sea for…well, we are not quite sure how long we have been here. We only know that the land of Fairendale, from which we were banished for reasons that are unimportant for this writing, always eludes us. But I am confident that we will find it soon.

Who are we? Well, we are pirates, and our story will be told in another annal that is not included in these you are currently reading. I will be the scribe who records our tale, but I must first learn how to write legibly on a rocking sea.

In any case, because you have been reading about mermaids with perhaps a bit of trepidation, allow me, someone who has actually encountered mermaids, to tell you a bit about them.

The most dangerous part of a mermaid is not her deceptive beauty but her song. When you are out on the open sea, there are many musical creatures who prey upon you. There are the musical twitters of the birds that would carry you off to another land (or so say the men on my ship—I have never seen this happen), and there are the musical groans of large creatures beneath the sea that would lure you into the depths, and then there are the musical songs of the mermaids bobbing on the surface waters.

Perhaps you have heard of the man who once tied himself to the bow of his ship when he knew he was passing a sea full of mermaids. This is because the song of a mermaid is quite intoxicating, and what their song says is, *Come to me.* And a man will do nearly everything he can to obey.

I must say that it is best not to venture near any waters where mermaids are known to be, but if you happen to find yourself in a problematic situation, here are some ways to protect yourself from the lure of mermaids.

1. Tie yourself to the ship.

This, of course, is not original in the slightest. But it is effective. You must, however, ensure that your knots are tied securely. There was once a man, not on my ship but on another we passed, who tied all the men of his crew to the ship and tied himself last. He had only one hand to tie the knots, and this was not an effective way to tie secure knots. Alas, he was lost among the waves of the sea. The only thing left of him was a brown boot that is said to mark the spot where he drowned, to this very day.

2. Stuff a stocking in your ear.

If it does not fit, keep shoving. Keep shoving until you can hear nothing else but the hum in your own head. Do not worry about extracting the sock once the danger of mermaids has passed. This will be a small worry in light of the fact that you are still alive.

3. Sing as loud as you can.

It does not matter if you have what is known as a bard's voice. When you pass the song of mermaids, you must sing as loud as you can to drown out their voices. There is a man on our crew who does not know how to carry a tune in the slightest. His singing is so terrible—a bellowing kind of sound like a thousand men croaking at the same time—that the mermaids flee when he opens his mouth. He is our most valuable crew member when the song of mermaids begins in the distance.

Sometimes you can beat the mermaids at their own game.

If you happen to fall for the charms of mermaids and find yourself flailing in the waters of the Violet Sea, well, there is no amount of kicking or screaming or otherwise struggling that will save you. This is because mermaids do not work alone. They work in hordes. If you break free from the three charming you above the surface, you can be assured that there are plenty more waiting beneath the depths.

As of yet, I have not tried out any survival techniques beneath the surface, as every man who has ever fallen for a mermaid has perished without a trace.

The Treaty Signed by King Sebastien, King of Fairendale,
and Zorag, Dragon King of Morad

On this third day of the the fourth month of the year
seventeen hundred and forty-nine, the people of Fairendale
and the dragons of Morad do hereby agree to the following:

All parties will remain on their side of the boundary line
between the Weeping Woods and their land.
Dragons in Morad, people in Fairendale.

Should anyone venture to cross, they will be sentenced to death.

Signed,

The Royal Family of Fairendale

King Willis: The current king of Fairendale. Has a deep love for sweet rolls, and it shows in his, well, wideness.

Queen Clarion: The current queen of Fairendale. Is underestimated by her husband, but we shall see just how powerful she is soon enough.

Prince Virgil: Son of King Willis and Queen Clarion, best friend of Theo. Prefers rye bread with melted butter to sweet rolls, depending on the day.

King Sebastien: Deceased king of Fairendale, exception to the line of boys who tried to steal thrones and were, upon failing at their quest, forever banished to sail the Violet Sea. Was killed by a blackbird.

The Villagers of Fairendale

Arthur: Village furniture maker and magic instructor to girls who possess the gift of magic. Is a bit reckless but always manages to come out on the other side—though one is not always assured it will be so.

Maude: Arthur's wife. Bakes spectacular pumpkin sugar cookies. Prefers caution to reckless abandon.

Hazel: Daughter of Arthur and Maude, twin of Theo. Cares for the village sheep and can even, amazingly, understand them.

Theo: Son of Arthur and Maude, twin of Hazel. Finishes his chores early so he can sit in on magic lessons.

Mercy: Daughter of Cora, best friend of Hazel. Prefers spectacular acts of magic to "boring" ones.

Cora: Mother of Mercy, widow, shape shifter. A woman who moves.

Garron: The town gardener. Talks to plants as though they can hear him. Has three sons: 12-year-old twins and a 13-year-old.

Bertie: The town baker. Enjoys showing off his air-kneading skills for the children.

Staff of Fairendale Castle

Garth: Page for King Willis, the oldest of twelve children. Sometimes calls King Willis "Your Wideness."

Cook: One of the few shape shifters in the land. Shape shifts into a bear. Is highly annoyed by her assistant, Calvin.

Calvin: An orphan who began working as Cook's assistant instead of traveling to live with distant relatives in Ashvale—and so did not perish in the Fire Mountain that claimed the entire population of Ashvale many years ago. Tasked with feeding the prisoners in the dungeons beneath the dungeons.

Sir Greyson: Captain of the king's guard. Receives medicine, which keeps his mother alive, in exchange for his service to the king. Carries a magical sword that cannot be lifted by any but him.

Sir Merrick: Second in command to Sir Greyson.

Important Prophets

Aleen: A prophetess who is one hundred forty-two years old, from the kingdom of White Wind. Wears ebony skin and what appears to be a collection of snakes for hair (though it is not).

Yerin: A prophet who is one hundred forty-two years old, from the wild woodland between Lincastle and Eastermoor. Has white hair that makes the dark of the dungeons where he is imprisoned a bit less dark.

Dragons of Morad

Zorag: King of the dragons of Morad. Lost his parents in the Great Battle, when King Sebastien stole the throne from the Good King Brendon. Would like nothing more than peace.

Blindell: Zorag's cousin, raised as the dragon king's son. Lost his parents in the Great Battle, when King Sebastien stole the throne from the Good King Brendon. Would like nothing more than revenge.

Larus: One of the elder dragons of Morad, male. Counselor to Zorag.

Malera: One of the elder dragons of Morad, female.

Counselor to Zorag.

The lost 12-year-old children of Fairendale

Ursula

Chester

Charles

Thumbelina (known as Lina among the children)

Minnie

Jasper

Frederick

Ruby

Martin

Oscar

Homer

Anna

Aurora

Rose

Edgar

Harriet (known as Hattie among the children)

Isabel (known as Izzy among the children)

Ralph

Dorothy

Julian

Tom Thumb

Philip

About the Author

While she has never possessed the gift of magic, L.R.'s teachers claimed she had a gift for words, which one might agree is quite like a gift of magic. Bringing a story to life that did not exist before is very much like transforming an old shoe into a dish towel. L.R. feels quite honored that she was given this gift and hopes to use it to encourage other young writers to discover their own gifts, for what is the world without words and stories?

L.R. is the queen of her castle in San Antonio, TX. She lives with her king and her six young princes, who daily give her inspiration for more grand tales of magic and adventure.

www.lrpatton.com

A Note From L.R.

I hope you've enjoyed reading this book from the annals of Fairendale's history. The world of Fairendale has been a lovely world to create, and I've had fun sketching maps, re-reading fairy tales and thinking, endlessly, about characters and their plights—because a series like this one takes lots and lots of time and hard work. But because it's always been my dream to create a fantasy world and share it with my readers, I knew it was something I had to do. (So, you see, dreams really do come true.)

If you have any questions about Fairendale or simply want to send me a note to tell me who your favorite character is or what kinds of extras you'd like to see me release in the future (a *Creatures of the Violet Sea* is coming soon!), email me at lr@lrpatton.com. I always enjoy hearing from my young readers.

Please consider leaving (or ask your parent to leave) a review of this book wherever you bought it. Reviews help get books into the hands of potential new readers, which is incredibly important for authors like me. And don't forget to pick up your free bonus materials when you stop by my web site! (www.lrpatton.com)

Thank you so much for supporting my work.

In love,

L.R.

Enjoy more stories from the magical Fairendale series:

LRPatton.com/Fairendale

Starter Library

Once upon a time...

The kingdom of Fairendale used to be the most peaceful in all the lands. Its people had never held a weapon before. And now they must, for the sake of the land. For the sake of their families. For the sake of their beloved king.

Read all about the king who had no heir, the girl who had magic, the dragon they loved, and the battle that changed everything in Fairendale's short story prequel, "The Good King's Fall."

Get it FREE, along with bonus materials "The Magical Rules of Fairendale" and "The Lands of Fairendale," for a limited time.

To get your FREE bonus materials, visit *
LRPatton.com/goodking

*Must be 13 or older to be eligible